MW01093408

© 2020 J T Daniels

This book is a work of fiction. Names, characters, places and incidents are products of this author's imagination or are used fictitiously. Any resemblance to actual events or locales or persons, living or dead, is entirely coincidental.

That being said, there is a real problem in the world of human trafficking. There are reports that it is a $32 billion-a-year business, with about one third of that coming from North America.
Less than 3% escape.

Cover photo: LisaHobbsPhotography.com

"May you never live in a darkness such as this."

— *J T Daniels*

Prologue

The little girl crouched in the tangled patch of thorns and briars, shaking. Her terror-filled eyes were wide. Her lips trembled. The matted, muddy mess of her blonde hair blended perfectly with the scraggly limbs of the brush around her. She was young. Five years old. But her survival instincts had been honed over the last few years. She knew she had to stay quiet. And small. Maybe, just maybe, Earl wouldn't find her. Maybe she could make it till morning. She crouched a little lower in the darkness. Just maybe.

Chapter 1

Gnaw Bone, Mississippi was a little podunk town that sat smack dab on the edge of the Mississippi Delta. To the east was the Delta, to the west, the hills and hollers. There were a few bars, most being run out of garages. And card games. There used to be a drive-in theater, but that burned down in the '80s. The skating rink had been taken over by hoodlums, drug dealers and the like. No decent person would dare go there after dark. There was a Kroger on one end of town and Walmart on the other. In between were about 15 churches. Southern Baptist, Protestant, Catholic, Pentecostal. Name the religion and there was a church for it in Gnaw Bone. Yes, sirree, southern folk liked their churches.

They also liked their liquor. And their drugs. Mostly crystal meth. Every once in a while someone would overdose with coke or heroin, but that usually happened with the college kids. What did they expect when they plopped a state college in a forlorn place like Gnaw Bone? Roses and sunshine? No! They get drugs, booze and religion. Anything to take their minds off this miserable little town.

The center of town was relatively nice. There was a town square with a small park and benches to sit and play checkers. Surrounding the square were little specialty shops that drew some tourists in. There was also a soap maker, a high-end dress shop, a '50s diner, a five-and-dime, an ice cream parlor, the police office, library, post office and a clinic. Magnolia trees lined the street and there was a statue of Confederate General Michael "Gnaw Bone" Fester, after whom the town was named. He was given the nickname of "Gnaw Bone" because of his habit of gnawing every bit of meat off the bones during dinner in camp. He claimed that if scraps still had meat, that was meat a starving union soldier might be able to eat to regain his strength. The currently politically correct trend of removing all Southern history had not yet reached much of the Deep South. So General Gnaw Bone still stood proudly in the square.

Just outside of the town square district were the nice homes of respectable people who worked at the college or somewhere in county seat of Cleveland, as Gnaw Bone had no industry. The farther one traveled outside the town square, the poorer the community. The edges were where the hookers and drug users congregate. This was where one would find the rough bars which cater to undesirable types. It was seedy, dirty and run down. It was like a shanty town, where most buildings were made of plywood, metal and even cardboard boxes. Here the vagrants gathered, huddled over small fires in old rusty barrels. A railroad ran nearby and hobos dropped in periodically. Those with money frequented the bars and whore house. Those who had no money sat around holding out cups, hoping for a little spare change.

The town had tried several times to clean up the shanty area, to no avail. It always sprang back.

Chapter 2

Faye Collier was from a good but poor family. Her daddy was a tractor mechanic and her mother worked in a tile plant. They made just enough to keep the family off the streets, but they were determined that Faye would be better. That meant graduating high school.

Faye had other ideas. She did well enough in school without trying too hard, but she had no friends. The other kids were all well off and tended to stick together. They hardly even noticed her in class. They noticed even less when she skipped class, which was a lot.

Faye was a good looking girl. Her strawberry blonde hair was long and silky. Freckles dotted her nose like powdered sugar on a cookie. She developed early and had the body of a centerfold model. Her eyes were crystal blue, like ice. No one at school knew how beautiful she was. Her daddy thought showing beauty was a sin. She had to wear droopy, baggy clothes that hid her figure and a scarf that covered her hair. When she skipped school, she would remove the scarf, but she had no other clothes to change into, so she still wore the oversized ones.

Her favorite hangout when she skipped school was Jimmy's drive-in. It was the kind where one parked, ordered from a speaker and girls in skimpy outfits on roller skates brought the order to the car. It was right next to the city park and all the kids with cars would cruise around and around the eatery when they got out of school. Faye could sit in the park and watch them in their shiny muscle cars and dream that *she* was in the front seat with the hot quarterback, ordering burgers and shakes.

One day, one of her classmates, Parker, circled the drive-in and noticed her sitting in the park. He parked and walked over to her. Parker was about 5'10" and thin. He had dark hair and liquid brown eyes. He was the placekicker of the high school football team.

"What 'cha doin'," he drawled.

"Just sittin' here," she answered.

She had caught Parker staring at her in class. He had never approached her and she had never acknowledged him. He kinda scared her a bit. The look in his eyes was a little mysterious. She didn't really know enough about the birds and bees to know what that look meant. So she just avoided him altogether. Besides, he ran with the popular crowd, in which she would never be accepted.

"You wanna share my shake?" he asked, pushing the frosty cup toward her. "Here, take a sip."

So she did. It was cold and creamy and chocolate.

They sat and talked a little while, until it began to get dark. The fireflies were coming out and the street lights had come on.

"Well, I gotta git home," she said, rising from the bench.

"Let me drive you," he offered.

"I don't think so. I don't live far," she blushed.

"Oh, come on! I want to show you somethin'," he insisted.

She felt a little butterfly in her tummy. "Well, okay," she said. "But I have to be home by ten or my daddy will kill me."

"No problem," he answered as he held open his door for her. Faye slid in.

Parker drove out to the lakeside just a little south of town. Turns out, the football team was having a bonfire before the big game tomorrow. The booze was flowing and the party was well underway. As they pulled up, half the team whooped and shouted for Parker to join them. They even seemed glad to see her, even though she was the only girl there. These bonding parties were for the team only, no girls allowed.

That was the first night she had felt accepted. She laughed and danced and drank quite a bit. It seemed as if every time her glass was empty, some jock would fill it up again. Not wanting to risk ridicule, she drank. And drank. And drank.

She barely remembered Parker leading her to the car and opening the back door. She barely remembered him thrusting himself into her, while the others watched and egged him on. She barely remembered the next four or five guys taking their turns. She passed out after the fifth guy.

She woke up on her front lawn, bloodied and torn. And, as she later found out, pregnant.

When she discovered she was pregnant, she told her mother about being raped.

"Mama, those boys held me down and made me do it!" she cried. "I couldn't stop them. I tried!"

"Now, Faye, you know nobody can make you do somethin' you don't wanna do. You just didn't fight hard enough. You should have known what was gonna happen when you went off with those boys. You should be ashamed of yourself."

"But, Mama, I didn't. I thought they liked me! Please don't tell Daddy!"

"I have to, Faye. We don't keep secrets in this house. Daddy's gonna be mad. Go to your room until he gets home."

She sat sobbing in her room, until she heard Daddy come through the front door. Then she heard him and Mama murmuring in low voices in the other room. Suddenly, Daddy burst through her bedroom door, red faced and angry as a hornet.

"You done got yourself pregnant?!" he yelled.

Faye shrank away from him.

Daddy raised his hand and smacked her hard on the shoulder. Not once, but several times. And then he kicked her out of the house with only the clothes she had on.

"No whore is goin' to live in my house!" he yelled as he slammed the door. Mama just stood in the background, sobbing and shaking her head. She would not go against her husband. Faye never spoke to them again. Sometimes she would sit outside their house, but she never approached the door. Daddy saw her once, when he came home from work. He stared at her sitting on the curb for just a moment before turning his back and going in. She never went back.

The kids at school had heard the rumor of her being pregnant. They made fun of her, bullied her and shamed her every chance they got. After a week or so, she dropped out of school and ended up waiting tables at Pizza Shack, working for tips only. The owner, Jerry, liked Faye. She was a looker with curves in all the right places. Especially wearing the revealing, skimpy uniform he required all his girls to wear. Low cut blouse tied up under the breasts to show the midriff with low, hip hugger Daisy Duke shorts that left little to the imagination. Faye wasn't showing yet so the uniform fit her perfectly. Plus, he liked 'em young. He was 40, bald, fat and single. He had pock marks all over his face, leftovers from his teenage years. Women didn't even glance at him anymore. So, here was a sweet young thing who knew her way around a man because she was knocked up and obviously needed help.

Jerry offered Faye a deal: move in and clean my house in exchange for rent. She jumped on it. It sure beat staying in the abandoned trailer in the back of the local gas station. She thought if she didn't have to pay rent and could save all her paycheck, she could save enough to move into her own place before the baby was born. She only had the few clothes she had kept in her school locker, which she brought with her when she moved in that night.

It was almost a week before Jerry raped her. He stumbled into her room after drinking all night. His sleeveless wife-beater t-shirt was covered in stains and sweat. He had on no pants, just his boxers. There was no gentleness, no foreplay. He liked it rough. He rolled off her when he was done and instantly began snoring. She crawled out of bed and cleaned herself up. She curled up with a blanket in the corner and cried herself to sleep. There would be no dreams tonight. Her dreams were all gone.

Jerry raped her every night until her belly got big. He just couldn't take the big, disgusting bump getting in his way. And her smell changed. It made him sick! But he had friends that had no problem with humping a pregnant chick. And they would pay. Faye was in no position to refuse.

Night after night, strange men came in. She got used to sleeping all day and being raped all night. It became her routine. All her dreams were dead, her future bleak and she accepted that. She gave birth to Jody in her room at Jerry's. Jerry was furious that she couldn't work for a while, but he didn't kick her out. He even took a liking to sweet little Jody.

Jerry died when Jody was a year old. Faye woke up to feed the child one night and tripped over his body laying in the hallway. Turned out, he had died from a massive heart attack.

She left him there for three days until she could no longer stand the smell. She called the local police and the hearse came and got him. Just like that, she was free.

As the years crawled by, Faye continued her routine. She still serviced men, but now she kept the money. She even began entertaining during the day. Jody would sit and watch cartoons while her mama was busy. Then they would go get McDonald's. Sometimes, they would eat at the park and she would let Jody play on the playground.

By the time Jody entered the fifth grade, her body had started to fill out. She had gorgeous, thick blond hair like her mama. Her breasts were small and pert. A narrow waist flowed into long, perfect legs. Her skin was flawless. All the boys were after her but she had no use for them. She had seen her mama with tons of men and she was determined not to head down that road. Even at the tender age of 11, she had a clear image of her future. It did not include men, sex or children.

By now, Faye was no longer the beauty she had been. Her breasts sagged and her looks had faded. Men would still visit her, but not as often and they didn't want to pay as much anymore. She was lucky if she made $100 in a night. She had gotten hooked on crystal meth and her habit was taking all her money.

Faye had noticed the changes in Jody's body. She began to resent her youth, her beauty. And money was tight, damn it! There's no reason that girl shouldn't be helping out. The men would pay top dollar for a girl that young. And she herself wouldn't have to work so hard. It would leave her more time to relax.

On Jody's twelfth birthday, Faye announced she was going to throw her a party that night. Jody was confused. They had never celebrated her birthday. She didn't have any friends to invite, but mama said she had something special planned. The anticipation built in her all day at school. She had never had a party before. She was so excited!

She ran home after school. As she burst through the door, she saw the balloons and ribbons streaming from the ceiling. Mama had cleaned the kitchen and baked a cake! And supper smelled so good. It was her favorite — fried chicken and mac and cheese! Tonight was going to be soooo special!

As they sat down to eat, Faye poured a tiny bit of her special "juice" for Jody. Jody lifted the glass to her lips nervously. Mama had never let her have even a sip before. She always said it would make her feel funny. But tonight was special, so Jody took a sip. It burned all the way to her tummy! She coughed and gasped for breath. Faye laughed out loud as Jody's eyes began to water.

"Hold, on it gets better," she said.

And it did. The burn slowly turned into a warm, buttery glow. Jody took another sip. It didn't burn as badly this time. She actually began to like it. Now she knew why Mama hadn't shared before. It was too special to share.

Faye filled her glass several times over the next hour while they ate. By the time she had cleaned her plate, she was very sleepy. She stood to leave the table, but her legs wouldn't work right. And her head was fuzzy. Mama helped her to the couch. There was a knock at the door.

"Honey," she said, "I have a special friend comin' over to spend some time with you tonight. You do whatever he says and everythin' will be alright. You take him to your room and y'all play nice. Okay?"

How could she say no? Mama had made her favorite food and shared her special juice. The evening had been so wonderful. She could surely be nice to Mama's friend. She would show him her dolls! And they could play. She could be nice.

"Sure, Mama," she said, slurring her words.

Mama opened the door and a man came in. He was old. Older than Mama even. He smiled and Jody saw he had several teeth missing. He had a big belly and scraggly, greasy hair. She thought that if he was that ugly, maybe he, too, had no friends. She felt sorry for him. She decided she would let him play with her favorite doll. That would make him feel better.

Jody slid off the couch and wobbled over to the man.

"Hi. I'm Jody," she said as she extended her hand. "Mama said we could play together in my room."

"Did she now?"

"I'm gonna let you play with my best doll! Come on!"

The man took her hand and they walked down the hallway to her room. Mama was smiling at her.

Jody stumbled over to her bed where all her dolls were. She hesitated a moment when the man closed her door. How would Mama know she was being nice if the door was closed?

"I'm gonna to let you play with my favorite doll tonight because you are Mama's special friend," she said sweetly.

"Oh, darlin," the man drawled, "I ain't here to play with no dolls."

As she sat there wide-eyed and puzzled, he removed his shoes and pants. Then he lay on the bed, dragging her on top of him. She struggled to get free and he held her tighter.

"No sense squirmin', darlin'. This is gonna happen. Your mama owes me money and I'm here to collect. So stay still and it'll go easier on ya."

Jody screamed. Something was wrong. Where was Mama? What was happening?

"Mama! Mama! Help me!"

No one came to help. The man ripped off her clothes and jammed his man part into her. It hurt so bad. She could feel her insides tearing. He bit her breasts until the skin broke. By the time he had finished, she was in shock. She didn't move. She didn't speak. She was somewhere else now. She was in the park, swinging. Nothing was hurting her.

She was barely aware of the man leaving. Mama came in and told her she had done good. The man was happy, but Jody didn't hear her. She was still in the park. It would be morning before she returned.

When she woke up the next morning, there were men in the living room waiting. One by one, they came to her room and raped her, while Mama sat at the kitchen table collecting their money.

That became her new life. No more school. By the time she was 14, men didn't come to see Faye anymore. They came for Jody. And she did not disappoint.

Faye had taught Jody all her tricks. With her youth and beauty, Jody brought in the men. They would line up outside the trailer, waiting their turn. She had the energy to go all night.

Jody demanded half the money when she realized how much Faye needed her. And Faye gave it to her. She was so pleased with the influx of cash, she was glad to share. Her body was gone. Her habit was out of control. And the girl was strong. She could work a long time. Just as long as she didn't get knocked up.

Chapter 3

By the age of 15, Jody was a bar rat hooked on crystal meth. No one knew she was pregnant. She hadn't gained but a couple of pounds and wasn't showing at all. Mama rarely paid attention to her as long as she brought home the money.

She gave birth in the backseat of her mom's beat up '82 Cavalier outside of the Joe's Booty Call bar. It didn't hurt too bad. The baby just slid out onto the seat. Afterwards, she used some old rags that were in the trunk to clean herself up. Mama would expect her to bring some money home and no guy was gonna pay to have sex with a bloody mess. Oh, well. Tonight it would just have to be blow jobs. She held her baby for a little while before wrapping her in the soft sweater she had worn and tucking her safe in the back floorboard. She slowly ambled into the bar to begin her night.

The night wasn't as profitable as she knew Mama thought it should be. The regulars were too engrossed in the football game to pay her any mind. Who could blame them? Football was big in this state and Ole Miss was on a tear this season. 8-0. But that didn't help her situation with Mama. She knew a beating was coming as soon as she got home.

As she fumbled with her keys, she could hear the baby crying. She instantly felt a strange sensation in her breasts. She didn't know much about babies, but she knew they needed to be fed. She remembered from that long ago health class that breast milk is best.

She gingerly picked her up and raised her to her breast. The precious little girl latched onto her nipple and began to nurse. It was at that moment, Jody knew love. The baby was perfect with her soft downy blond hair and her tiny pink lips.

Jody was afraid of Mama. Faye had been hooked on drugs so long, that was all she thought about. That and money. Mama had warned her many times not to get pregnant. She could be real mean if Jody didn't bring home enough to feed her habit. She would beat her mercilessly as she had many times before. Even though she knew it was unlikely, Jody hoped Mama wouldn't be too mad. She hoped the baby would bring some joy into both their lives.

When the child seemed sated and fell asleep, she wrapped her up and lay her gently in the floor again. She even hummed a little tune as she drove down the dirt road to Highway 61.

Faye sat in her dingy kitchen, a cloud of smoke hanging over her head, permeating every fabric in the room. Years of smoking had turned the walls a dirty yellow. The linoleum table she sat at was cracked with age. The light hanging over the table was a single bulb, heightening the gloom of the wretched little room.

Her hair had lost its shine long ago. The meth had taken all but three of her teeth. Her eyes were no longer sparkling and the only thing she looked forward to was her next fix.

She no longer thought of Jody as anything but a money machine. The girl had made more money than Faye had in her best years. But Faye ran through it as fast as Jody could earn it. She was late tonight. That girl had better not be out giving it away for free!

Jody pulled up in the driveway and killed the lights. Praying Mama was in a good mood, she picked up her precious bundle and opened the door.

"Hey, Mama!" she said.

"Don't hey me," Mama grumbled without looking up. "Where's my money?"

"Well, I only got $40," she said in a low voice. "But, I brought you a present!"

"I don't need no damn present!" Faye bellowed. "I need my money!"

Jody held out the bundle. Faye grabbed it roughly and pulled the sweater back.

"A baby! A damn baby! What am I gonna to do with this?!" she yelled. "Is this yours?! How many times have I warned you to not get pregnant, you little bitch!"

But her face had softened. As she looked at the tiny little girl, her forehead relaxed. The baby was perfect, full of promise. But Faye knew promises were empty. This baby didn't benefit her in any way. Her face hardened again.

"Why did you bring this home? It's bad enough I have to feed you. I cain't feed no baby, too. It can't stay."

She lay the baby on the couch and stormed off to her room, fuming. Jody picked up her child and slowly walked down the hallway to her room. At least, Mama hadn't beat her. Not yet.

Faye did not sleep well that night. She needed money. She had to have her crystal meth. Life would be unbearable without it. An idea began to form. What if she traded the baby for drugs? After all, the child would have a better life, right? Any place was better than this. And she knew just the guy to see.

Faye rolled out of bed the next morning on a mission. She sneaked into Jody's room. The baby was laying on the floor next to the bed, all cozy in blankets. Just as she reached down to pick her up, Jody stirred.

"What's goin' on?" she murmured. "Where are you takin' her?"

"Just go back to sleep, sweetie," Faye whispered. "I'll take care of her."

Jody rolled over went back to sleep.

Faye took the child and lay her gently in the back seat of the car. As she pulled out of the driveway, she thought things were finally going to go her way.

Chapter 4

Earl Fields was raised hard. His mama and daddy were lifelong sharecroppers in the hot, sweaty cotton fields of the Delta. He was the fourth of nine kids and the only son. Every day was a fight for food, water, space, life. And Daddy did not spare the rod. He would beat him with a belt, board, iron skillet, whatever was handy. Most times, Earl had to pick out his own switch for the whooping. He learned to enjoy the pain. At least he had Daddy's attention when he was being beaten.

And the sex! Whoo-whee, there was a lot of sex in that little house. Daddy raped Mama nearly every night. There was no privacy in their one room sharecropper's shack. Mama had once hung a tattered quilt of burlap cotton sacks to hide her bed area, but Daddy had torn it down. He liked for the kids to watch. Knowing there was an audience bolstered his performance. The girls always looked away, cowered in the corner, sobbing and covering their ears. But, Earl was fascinated with the variety of torture Daddy used on Mama. He always inched as close as he could get so he didn't miss anything. Sometimes, Daddy let him help hold her down. Sometimes, he got to hand Daddy the pliers, knife, whatever instrument Daddy had chosen to use that night. Sometimes, he just sat and watched. And learned. It didn't bother him that Mama was pleading for mercy. He had learned long ago to ignore anything that didn't help him directly. In fact, he liked the pleading. It made it more exciting to him.

On one special night, Daddy declared that Earl, who was twelve, was now a man and could do man things. Daddy jerked Mary Lou, his sixteen year old daughter, off the dirty floor and threw her on his and Mama's bed. He tied her hands and feet to the bedposts using bailing string, just like he always did with Mama. Mary Lou, however, was not as submissive as Mama. She screamed and cried and jerked like a wild cat caught in a trap. Daddy had to punch her a couple of times to quiet her down. But the resistance only made Earl harder.

He then called Earl over and handed him a jar of homemade moonshine. Earl took a big swig, just like he'd seen Daddy do. His face turned bright red and his eyes teared up so fast, he couldn't see. He grabbed his throat and started coughing and sputtering. Daddy was laughing so hard he fell off the mattress. After a few minutes, Earl was able to see straight and reached for another swig. Daddy slapped him on the back and handed him the jar. "That's my boy!" he yelled. "Now, git over here and let's have some fun!"

From that night on, Earl owned the world and everything in it. He picked his share of cotton during the day, and reaped terror on his sisters at night. He enjoyed the way they cringed when he walked past, never knowing which one would be the chosen one. Never knowing which tool he would pick. Would it be the hammer? The carrot peeler? Or had he found something new in the shed?

When Earl was fourteen, he decided to run away. He had grown tired of the games with his sisters. They no longer resisted and submission had no appeal for him. He needed more stimulation. Daddy no longer participated. He just sat near the bed and drank himself to oblivion, watching with his beady eyes. Mama had died in her sleep the night he had first raped Mary Lou two years ago. So, it was time to move on.

That night, he waited till Daddy had passed out and the sisters were all asleep. He quietly padded over to the coffee can on the shelf above the stove where Daddy kept his liquor money. It wasn't much. Maybe twenty dollars. But just enough to get him down the road. As he replaced the can, Daddy stirred and opened his eyes. He was just sober enough to realize what Earl was doing. He reached his arm toward his son just as Earl's foot slammed into his face, snapping his scrawny neck.

Earl watched as Daddy fell back, his head at an odd angle. He moved closer to watch Daddy's face. Daddy's eyes had rolled back into his head. Spit and blood dribbled down his stubbly chin. His breath was shallow and reeked of chew and moonshine. Earl listened to the ragged breaths until there were no more. It was then that he realized his true power.

He took the oil lamps and poured the kerosene all over the floor, the bed and the walls. As he walked out the door, he dropped the match. He could hear his sisters' screams as he ambled leisurely down the dirt road to Highway 61. He was ready for his new chapter. He was truly a man.

Earl hitchhiked to Memphis, where he stayed for several long years. Memphis is a hotbed of blues music and chicken joints. Beale Street is where all the tourist crowd goes. It is the glitzy, tame side of the blues world. Nothing ever happens there because there are cops all up and down the street. They are there to protect the tourist trade. However, two blocks off Beale Street is the real blues district. Bars are crowded with the working class or unemployed drinking moonshine and fighting. This cesspool is where Earl landed a job as a bouncer. He was busy every night, stopping fights, throwing people out into the street. Sometimes, he got a little overzealous and the drunk ended up with extra cuts or bruises, but only if they mouthed off to him.

His other skills he saved for the whores he took home. No one questioned if a whore came up hurt or, better yet, dead. Cops didn't really investigate and pimps just replaced her with another girl futilely looking for a career in music.

He eventually became an enforcer for a loan shark. His boss put no restrictions on how he collected the overdue money, so he was free to use his more brutal talents. He never killed anyone he was collecting from and he never had to pay a visit to the same person twice.

Earl didn't like drugs. He didn't want anything to dull his senses. He liked feeling everything. Even pain. So he didn't like drugs. But he saw the money his boss was raking in every week from dealing crystal meth. And he wanted in. But Memphis was too big. There was too much competition from the big boys in town.

He needed some place smaller where he could rule the trade. And he knew just the place. Gnaw Bone was about fifty miles from where he grew up. It was a crappy little town with only one police officer. Lots of hills and hollers to hide a lab in. And plenty of customers.

He bought an old run down shack a few miles out of town at the end of a dirt road. There was two rooms and a bathroom. Electricity didn't reach that far out, so Earl used a generator to pump water, watch television and run a refrigerator. He kept extra cans of gasoline for the generator out beside the shed.

There were a few meth heads that lived in run down places on the road leading to his house, but basically it was secluded with nothing else for miles around.

He worked in the local cotton mill ten hours a day. Such hard work had crafted his body into a lean, hard, toned machine. The mill didn't pay much, but he didn't mind. He needed a legitimate income to cover up his illicit business.

He had searched every inch of his land when he moved in. There were hills and valleys, all covered in brush and kudzu. It was difficult terrain that would deter nosy busybodies. He had found a cave deep in a holler that was perfect for a lab. Slaves had once hidden there before beginning their dangerous journey north.

There was brush and a big boulder concealing the entrance which made it unlikely a casual observer would spot the cave. There was a hole in the top of the cave that provided ventilation, although not enough to be safe. Earl wore an oxygen tank and mask while working. In the corner of the cave was a small generator which provided enough power for the cook. It takes about two days to make enough crystal meth for thousands of doses. He made a batch about once a month. Sooner if business demanded it.

He also started selling women when he was 23. One of his acquaintances from Memphis had approached him with a proposal. All he had to do was find a girl, reasonably good looking, no family and bring her to the man. No questions asked. He'd make an easy thousand bucks. Earl had found that many addicts in this part of the country would do just about anything for a hit. Sometimes he would use them for his own perverted pleasure in return for a little crystal. Before long, he was taking and selling girls to customers from all over the Deep South. The girls came easily. They were willing to do whatever he said for the drugs he offered free of charge. They didn't ask what would happen to them or where they were going. They didn't care. Not as long as he helped them out. No one ever caught him. No one ever came asking questions. Yet, everyone knew.

The flesh trade proved to be a nice business for him. It didn't interfere with his crystal business and sometimes he could sell both to the same customer. By far, drugs were his most lucrative venture, though. He had most of the Delta covered and would not tolerate anyone trying to cut into his business.

Chapter 5

Ah, the morning air was already heavy with humidity. It was early, but the sun had been beating down on his metal tin roof for several hours now and the house was heating up. Sitting on the porch trying to catch a breeze, Earl recognized the car careening up his dirt driveway. Ah, Faye needs another fix. He smiled. Faye knew every way to please a man and didn't cower away from the cruel things he liked to do to women. But she was getting old. She had no fight left and that didn't do it for him. He liked his women lively. Yep. This time she was gonna need money. No more trades for her.

Faye just marched right up to the porch with a dirty bundle of rags in her arms.

"I need a fix, Earl. I ain't leavin' till I get it," she declared.

"Well, Faye," he drawled. "How much money you got?"

"Well, that's the problem, ya see," she mumbled. "I ain't got no money."

He turned to go back inside.

"Go home, Faye," he spat. "No more trades for you. Send Jody around. Maybe she can pay for you."

"Wait!" she screamed. "I got somethin' better!"

She held the little bundle out to him.

"I bet you can fetch a pretty penny for her," she said, leering at him.

He pulled the cover back and saw this perfect, newborn little girl. A baby! What the hell did he need a baby for? His customers wanted girls, some as young as ten, but no one had asked for a baby. Yet.

"What am I gonna do with a baby?!" he yelled. "This ain't no daycare!"

"Aw, come on, Earl. Everyone knows you sell things. And this baby is perfect! You could get a lot for her," she insisted.

He considered her offer for a minute. Faye was jonesing hard. He knew she would do anything for the next fix.

"I tell you what, Faye," he said. "You give me Jody and I'll take the child, too. If you do that, you can have all the meth you want."

Faye seemed perplexed. How was she going to live without Jody bringing in money? She thought a moment. Her trailer was paid for, so no rent. She could use her food stamps on herself instead of her and Jody. And Earl was going to give her free drugs. She couldn't see a downside to this deal.

"I can do that," she replied.

"Good. Just one thing. Jody has to agree. I can't have her tryin' to run away all the time."

"Oh, she'll agree. I'll see to it," Faye chuckled. "I'll bring her around today. Meantime, keep the kid. It'll make it easier to get Jody to go along."

After Faye left, Earl lay the child in the bedroom on the tattered quilt that covered his bed. This is going to work out great, he thought. He had wanted Jody for a long time. She had always refused to service him. Word had spread and all the girls knew that Earl played rough. Jody didn't go in for that kind of stuff. It just fueled his desire.

Although he traded in women, he had no intention of selling Jody. It had been hard lately getting women to agree to his kind of foreplay. But with Jody, he had leverage. That baby laying on his bed ensured she would do whatever he wanted. For as long as he wanted. Oh, yes. This deal was going to work out well for him.

Faye drove straight home, excited to get this thing rolling.

"Jody! Jody, get up!" she yelled as she flung the trailer door open.

She almost ran down the hallway to Jody's room. The twit was still asleep. She jerked the covers off and grabbed her by the arm, pulling her off the bed.

"What the hell?" Jody cried. "What is goin' on?"

Wide awake now, she looked around for the baby.

"Where's Tess?" she screamed. "Where's my baby?!"

Faye slapped her.

"Now, listen here, girl," she said in a low, menacing voice. "I am givin' you to Earl Fields. You and that baby. I ain't got no more use for you. And you are gonna to stay with him! No runnin' away. Ain't no place for you to go."

Jody sat in a heap, weeping.

"Mama, why? Why you doin' this?" she asked.

Faye watched her sobbing like a pathetic weakling. She saw the rebellion swell up in Jody. Jody looked up at her, eyes glittering, face hard.

"I ain't doin' it," she said. "I'll go to Tunica. Get me and Tess a place to live. You can't give me away! I'm a human bein'! I'm your daughter and Tess is your granddaughter! You can't give us away!"

Faye's hands balled up into hard fists. She jumped on Jody like a tiger, pounding her as hard as she could. She hit her everywhere but her face. Earl might renege on the deal, if Jody showed up all bruised and swollen.

"You ARE gonna to do this," she growled in Jody's ear. "If you don't, he will kill that brat and then he will kill you. You hear me? Run away and he will chase you down and gut your little girl before he guts you! Now get your ass up and pack your things. We gotta go."

Jody didn't have much to pack. A few clothes for herself and a few things she had managed to buy secretly for the baby when she was pregnant. She had kept those hidden from Mama. But now, she threw all of it into a bag and trudged out to the car.

Mama was waiting. They didn't speak on the way to Earl's. Jody couldn't figure out why Mama had done this. She had been making plenty of money to keep the drugs flowing. Surely, merely having a baby didn't cause this. She wanted to ask her again. But she didn't. She just sat, cowered against the door, whimpering.

Earl was on his porch as they drove up the road. The old Cavalier had seen better days and made quite a racket. He could see Faye hunched behind the wheel. There was no sign of Jody. He wondered if the old hag had screwed up.

The car stopped and Faye jumped out.

"Okay, I got her. Now give me my drugs," she cackled.

Earl just looked at her. Hard.

"I don't see no Jody, Faye," he said.

Faye whirled around and stomped to the passenger side. She jerked open the door and grabbed Jody, dragging her from the car. Jody struggled to get away from her and stood up. She kept her eyes down, looking furtively for a way to escape.

"She don't look very cooperative, Faye," Earl said. His voice was low now, dangerous.

"Don't you worry, Earl," Faye replied. "She knows her place. She'll do what you want."

Earl looked Jody up and down, slowly licking his lips. Jody stared back at him defiantly.

"Git in the house, Jody," he said. "Tend to your baby."

At the mention of the baby, Jody looked up. So that was it. Mama had traded her and her baby for drugs! She should have known.

Jody slowly trudged up the steps and in the house, inching as far away from Earl as she could get. She heard Tess in the bedroom and hurried to her. She picked her up and hugged her tightly, crying uncontrollably.

"Don't worry, little Tess," she sobbed. "I'll get us out of this." She rocked her until Tess quieted.

Outside, Faye looked at Earl defiantly, as if to say, "I held up my end. Now it's your turn."

Earl sighed and reached in his pocket. He handed Faye a small bag of crystal meth. She grabbed it and turned to go.

"That's a week's worth, Faye," he said. "Don't come back before the week's done. You hear?"

Faye paid him no mind. She was already in the car and heading home. Bliss awaited.

Earl walked slowly back into the house. He could see Jody sitting on the bed feeding the baby. The sight of the tiny little girl suckling at Jody's soft white breast excited him. He had a little time before he had to go to town for business. May as well get Jody in line right off the bat.

She saw Earl had standing in the doorway, watching her feeding Tess. The look on his face told her something bad was coming. Jody lay the child down and began buttoning up her blouse. Earl took one long step and jerked her up off the bed.

"No need for that, Jody," he whispered. "Time to play."

He grabbed her wrist and dragged her to the kitchen. With one swoop of his long arm, he wiped the table clear and threw her on the table. Her kicking and scratching didn't slow him down one bit. He laughed as he held her arms with one of his hands and used his leg to keep her legs still.

"You're gonna to enjoy this, Jody. It's been a long time comin'," he drawled.

He ripped her shirt off. She wasn't wearing a bra, so her breasts were fully exposed. He squeezed them. Hard. He lowered his mouth and lapped the dribble of milk that came out. Hmm, he thought. This was a new twist. He licked it again. Yes, this was definitely new.

Her skimpy little shorts came off with one jerk. Now she was completely naked and at his mercy. Since he was pressed for time, there would be no fun stuff. He loosened his throbbing manhood from his jeans. He was harder than he'd been in a long time. Jody's fighting him reminded him of his sisters before they became compliant.

He rammed himself into her. She screamed. It wasn't as if she wasn't used to this. But this was different. This was primal. Having just given birth last night and been beaten by her mother today, her body had reached its limits. The pain was unbearable. But still she fought.

When he was done, he stood up, adjusting his clothes. He watched her jump off the table. She faced him, defiantly, clutching her fists to her side. He knew he had hurt her, but didn't care. She was his. Might as well get used to it.

Earl grabbed his keys off the wall and walked to the door. He said, over his shoulder, "Have supper ready when I get back."

Then he looked at her with disgust.

"And clean yourself up. You smell."

Then he was gone.

Chapter 6

Earl had been really busy since Jody and the baby had come. Casinos had finally opened in Tunica and his meth business had tripled. He was gone for days at a time.

Jody settled into a routine of taking care of the baby. She loved playing house with Tess. She would take her on long walks around the property, down the gullies, across the crick, into the woods. Tess liked to sit in the crick and play in the water. Her little face would crinkle up in laughter as the tiny minnows darted all around her. She tried to catch them by slapping at the water. They would shoot out in all directions and she would just about fall over giggling.

Faye would come around sometimes, looking for Earl and drugs. Jody never answered the door when Earl wasn't there. That was the number one rule. She only answered a few times when she knew it was Faye. Faye had seemed to not recognize her. It was as if they were total strangers. So she quit answering the door altogether.

Jody thought about running when Earl was gone. She thought she would take Tess and make her way to Memphis. But she remembered Earl's threat to gut her baby and then her and she had no doubt he would carry out that threat. He knew people everywhere all the way to Memphis. All he had to do was put out the word and she would be caught. There was no hope of escape. No place to hide. All she could do was make the best of life while he was gone. And try to survive it when he was home.

She had discovered a trap door under the rug in the kitchen. It opened into a small dirt root cellar. The space was about 4'x6' and completely empty. As she climbed down the rickety ladder, she felt a sudden calm descend upon her. It was dark and cool down there. The quiet just enveloped her like a warm blanket. She felt safe. That's when the idea hit her. This could be a safe haven for Tess while Earl played his games with her. It could shield Tess somewhat from the horror Jody lived with.

She began by covering the dirt floor with an old quilt she had found in the bedroom closet. Whoever had lived in the shack before Earl had left behind nearly all their household goods. She took one of the 2"x4" boards from the back yard and wedged it in place near the back of the cellar. She filled the space between the board and the dirt wall with blankets and pillows, creating a bed of sorts, perfect for a small child. She put a flashlight, bottled water and some crackers in a small box and tucked it away in the corner.

Tess had no toys. Jody hadn't had a chance to get any before arriving at Earls and she hadn't left his house since that day. She took an old dishcloth and spread it on the table. She then wadded up a piece of paper and draped the cloth over the paper. She took a shoelace from her shoe and tied it beneath the ball of paper to form a head. The finishing touch was using a marker to make eyes and a smiling mouth. As she looked over her work, she smiled. It wasn't a real doll, but she was proud of what she had done. She placed the doll on the makeshift bed. At least Tess would have company during playtime.

Earl had paid no attention to Tess since they had been there. When he came home, he would eat, sleep and rape Jody. He liked having someone to come home to. Someone to be at his beck and call. Someone to defy him. Jody was good at that. No matter what he did to her, she fought. She had been there over a year now and she still had fire in her blood. As long as he had the brat, he had her.

As he pulled up to the shack, he was hornier than usual. He had been gone all week, pushing his meth in Tunica, screwing whores and gambling. The whores were no fun. They didn't fight or scream. He may as well of been with a corpse. He had also lost at gambling, which fueled his rage. He was looking forward to having some fun with Jody.

Jody saw his truck coming up the driveway. There was no mistaking that vehicle. It was huge and black. The windows were tinted so dark, anyone inside was hidden. It had big glass pack pipes that roared so loud people from miles around could hear it. That truck was a point of pride with him. Complete with gun rack and Winchester hunting rifle.

She grabbed Tess and a bottle of milk and crept as fast as she could down the ladder. She settled Tess in the bed, gave her the bottle, turned on the flashlight and raced back upstairs. She had just gotten the kitchen table back in place when Earl stepped onto the porch. She sat down and waited.

He broke through the door like a bull in a china shop. She could see he was angry. His eyes were hard and glittery. If she didn't know better, she would say he was high on his own meth. But Earl didn't use. He always said that was for losers. So he must have lost money somehow. Whatever it was, she knew she was going to pay.

He walked right up to her and punched her in the gut. She bent over in pain, but did not cry out. He jerked her out of the chair by the hair and dragged her into the bedroom. She didn't want to scare Tess by screaming, so she just kicked and scratched at him. If Tess got scared and cried, that would draw Earl's attention. That was the one thing she did not want. She wanted all his attention on her.

He splayed her out on the bed, tying her wrists and ankles to the bedposts before ripping her clothes off. Spread-eagled like that, she could only writhe helplessly. She watched as he took a cloth roll out of his dresser drawer. She hadn't seen it before, but, then, she didn't really go rummaging around in his stuff anymore. He would always know she did and punish her.

He glanced at her as he unrolled the tool pouch. He had not yet used tools on her. He wondered if she would still be silent. Would this make her lose her fight? That would be a shame.

He held up the small carving knife. He rubbed it against his thumb and watched her as a thin rivulet of blood ran down. He raised his thumb to his mouth and slowly licked the blood, keeping his eyes on Jody. He could see she was afraid. He wondered if she would go all weak on him now. He hoped not.

He sat on the bed and began running his fingers over her skin. He could feel her shrink away. So far, she hadn't said anything. No begging, no crying. He touched the knife to her belly. A tiny speck of blood appeared. He grinned as he lowered his head to lick the blood keeping his eyes locked with hers.

Suddenly, Jody bucked, striking her hip bone into his cheek. He laughed. Here was the spirit he loved.

He stood and removed his clothes. He straddled her on the bed, knife in hand. He began making tiny little cuts all over her body. They were shallow. No deeper than a paper cut. But with every one, she writhed and bucked and grunted. Still no cries or screams. The tears were flowing, though. And the look in her eyes told him more than any scream could. She was in hell. He laughed again.

He raped her when he was done with the knife. When he finally untied her so he could sleep, she crawled off the bed and curled up on the floor until she could breathe. It had been near impossible to keep from screaming, and yet, she had done it. Tess had heard nothing.

This was the first time he had cut her. Before, he had hit her, pinched her, raped her with bottles, but no blood letting. Tonight had been different. His rage was growing and she didn't know how to avoid it. She knew that tonight was a turning point. From here on out, it would get worse. Much worse.

Chapter 7

Earl was sitting at Joe's Booty Call one night nursing his drink. He didn't know how many he'd had and didn't care. He'd been in Tunica the past week and life was good. He was raking in the money selling meth and girls to the casino crowd. His home life was good, too. Jody cooked and cleaned. She was also there for his, um, unique desires. And she took care of the brat so well, he barely knew it was there.

So why did he feel as if he were about to explode? That tense energy that builds up inside when something is wrong was growing stronger. He had felt someone watching him in Tunica. He hadn't seen them, but his gut told him danger was afoot. Some of his customers had been unusually cordial to him, as if they were distancing themselves from him. He felt something was going on, but couldn't figure out what it was. No one would dare encroach upon his territory, so it had to be something else.

As he sat brooding over his whiskey, a young, black man slid onto the stool beside him. He was well groomed. His expensive three-piece Italian suit was definitely out of place in Joe's. His black patent leather shoes had just been shined. He pulled a gold cigarette case from his breast pocket and offered Earl a cigarette. Earl waved him off. He didn't need a slick gambler getting close. He didn't know this man and wasn't about to trust a stranger.

The man chuckled. His voice was rich and throaty. He had a British accent. Or maybe it was South African. One thing Earl knew for sure. It definitely wasn't local. His smile was wide as he lit his cigarette. A gold tooth glittered.

He glanced up from his cigarette and surveyed Earl. He saw a egotistical, arrogant hillbilly. Someone who bullied his way to the top. The man was disgusted.

"I come with a message from Tunica," he said. "They are going to be taking over your business there. I am here to politely suggest you take your goods elsewhere. You are no longer welcome in Tunica."

Earl slowly turned his head to stare at the man.

"And just who is 'they'," he asked.

"Concerned parties," the man replied. "Parties you don't want to know. You should take their advice."

"And if I don't?"

"Well, it's my job to press upon you how serious my clients are. If you don't listen, they won't be so nice. So what do you say? Cease and desist and you'll never see me again," he whispered as he rose and stubbed out his cigarette.

"I tell you what," Earl said as he, too, rose from his stool. "You tell them I don't lay down for no one. If they want..."

The man had moved so quickly and smoothly, Earl hadn't even noticed the silver blade. It slipped in and out of his side, like butter. The man turned and walked out of the bar. Earl sat down for a split second before slowly sliding off the barstool onto the floor. He could feel the blood pooling on the floor beneath him. As he faded, he could hear someone yelling, "Call 911!" His last thought was "What the hell?" and then he was out.

He woke up in the hospital three days later. Loss of blood had put him in a coma. The nurse said they had to resuscitate him four times during surgery. He had actually died and been brought back! He didn't remember. What happened to the light everyone talked about?

He was the worse patient in the hospital. He called the nurses whores and bitches. "Bitch bring me some water." "Hey, whore! I need pain killers." "Bitch, some sit on my lap. Little Earl needs kissed."

The doctors were men, so he wasn't quite so rude with them. He needed them on his side if he were to get out of here anytime soon.

He had physical rehab every day and despised every moment. With rehab, he was constantly reminded of his weakness.

The knife had nicked one of his arteries. He also had weakness on his left side, so he when left the hospital a month later, he left with a cane. And a foul, dark mood.

Jody had healed somewhat over the last month or so while Earl had been gone. When the day came that she heard his truck from a mile away, her shoulders dropped. She grabbed Tess and hugged her tightly.

When he opened the truck door to get out, she noticed something was wrong. Why was he moving so slow? He looked older. And meaner, if that was possible. He had a scowl she had never seen before. Oh, yes, something was horribly wrong. Things were gonna get real bad. She hugged the child closer to her body. Heaven help us, she thought.

Earl hobbled up the porch steps, glaring at her. What was she gawking at? He was still strong, still in charge. He brushed past her and then stopped. He turned to face Jody. Was this child she was holding the same one he had left in her care? On the few times he'd been home before the stabbing, he had not noticed the child. But, this! This child he liked. Soft curly blonde hair, blue eyes and pretty pink lips. Oh, yes! This one would be a beauty. Men would pay a very high price for her.

He reached out and stroked Tess' cheek. So soft! Jody slapped his hand away. He snickered and went inside.

"Make me some dinner, whore!" he shouted. "That hospital food is crap."

Jody lay Tess down in the bedroom floor on a pallet of blankets and pillows and hurried to scrounge up some food. As she fixed Earl a ham sandwich, she pondered what could have happened to put him in the hospital. He most likely had lost a fight. Over what, she didn't know. Probably drugs. She didn't dare ask him. It would only remind him he had lost and he would take it out on her. She arranged his sandwich and a beer on a tray and took it to him. She set it down on the table in front of the sofa. Earl grabbed the tail of her shirt and pulled her down into his lap.

"Little Earl needs some attention, little girl. He's been lonely all this time." The he shoved her face down in his lap.

"Get to it," he demanded, as he picked up his ham sandwich.

After Earl had passed out on the sofa later that night, Jody gathered Tess and packed a few things in a bag. She had seen the way he looked at Tess. Jody knew she could bear his torture, but Tess would never survive. Her only choice was to leave. Maybe she could make it out to the highway before Earl realized they were gone. Someone could give them a ride and she would be done with this place. Maybe she could get to Arkansas. She didn't think Earl had connections there.

They had walked about a mile before she heard the truck start up. She hurried to hide in the kudzu covering the trees and bushes on the roadside. She crouched there, trembling, and holding on to a sleeping Tess.

Earl had turned on the big hunting lights so everything in front of the truck was bathed in light. She lay flat on the ground and held her breath. The truck rolled slowly by and kept going. She waited a few more minutes before standing up. She couldn't continue down the road because she knew he would be coming back. The woods were thick and thorny. They were impassable, especially with a baby. Her only option was to cut through the cotton field and try to make it to the truck stop on Highway 61. They could get a ride there.

Jody picked up Tess and started to trudge through the field. It was slow going because the ground was muddy from the rain earlier in the day. The field was huge. The lights from the truck stop were tiny pin pricks on the horizon.

It seemed as if hours passed. She was about halfway through the field when she heard a low hum. Mosquitoes and other buzzing bugs were thick at night, but she didn't remember ever hearing a hum. As the sound grew louder, she realized it was his truck. She whirled around just as his lights came in view. He was headed straight for her, crushing everything in his path.

Terrified, she began running. Right away, she realized how futile it was. He was going to catch her. Maybe she could save Tess. She lay Tess, still sleeping, next to the nearest leg of the giant circle irrigator. It was out of his path and Tess would be safe. She kissed her forehead and began running in the opposite direction. She stumbled and fell face first in the mud.

He was close now. She wasn't going to make it. So, she stopped and turned to face Earl. Whatever he did to her, Tess would be safe. Someone would find her and she would be safe.

The truck stopped. It sat there in the field facing her, like a wild beast. He revved the engine and made the beast jump toward her. She fell to her knees. Her punishment would be severe, but she would survive. After a while, she would try again. She only hoped she had saved Tess from this monster.

Earl jumped down from his truck and walked slowly toward her. She was cowering like a trapped animal. He hated weakness. What happened to her fight? Her will to live? It just fueled his rage. She was no good to him like this.

He grabbed the rope from the back and stormed toward her. He tied the rope around her ankles, too tight. The whole time she was crying and mewling and begging. It made him sick. The only time she stopped her incessant whining was when he tied the other end of the rope to the rear bumper of his truck. Yeah, she was scared now. Now he would see some fight.

Jody was truly petrified. She knew he was cruel, but surely he didn't intend to kill her. For the split second she had left, she tried to think of ways to save herself. There were none. She thought of Tess, the only one who had ever loved her. She hoped Tess would remember her. For the first time in her life, she prayed. She prayed she would survive and she prayed someone would save Tess.

Earl revved his engine and took off across the field. He could see her in his rear view, just bouncing and flopping. It didn't take long for her to stop screaming. There was no fight left in her now.

Jody hadn't lasted long. Her head had hit the dirt furrows a couple of times before she got dizzy. She felt her legs break as she was jerked in unnatural ways. She passed out from the pain and never woke up. Her last thought was of Tess.

He pulled up next to the irrigator to untie the ropes. He threw what was left of her body in the bed of his truck. The ravines and wild animals would swallow it up. Now that his rage had subsided, he regretted killing her. He would have to find someone else with the same spirit to take her place. Damn her! Why did she make him do this?! He was about to get behind the wheel when he heard a cat meowing. The meowing turned into a full fledged bawl. Surely she's not still alive! He turned back to check. There was no movement.

That's when he saw something moving near the irrigator. The little bitch had tried to save the child! Joke's on her, though. He scooped up the toddler and tossed her in the truck.

Then Tess' hell began. She was three years old.

Chapter 8

Earl had gotten the message loud and clear. No more selling meth in Tunica. He was reminded of it everyday by the stabbing pain in his side and the pathetic, weakness in his arm. No, that business was done. He'd always thought of himself as a brave man, although, in reality, he was just too stupid to know better. But he did not want to mess with the people in Tunica. They were part of a bigger group and they would kill him next time.

Occasionally he got a girl to sell. But, the word was out and his high-rolling Tunica clients no longer looked to him for girls either. That business was all but dead, too. So, all he had was his local meth clients.

Earl was an angry man. He felt as if he had returned to his early boyhood when he had no power. His body was no longer reliable. He wanted people to fear him. But who could fear a weak, powerless man?

All the pain and self pity manifested into a burning rage. He knew one person who would fear him. The child.

He kept her chained in the kitchen most of the time. He would toss her scraps occasionally just out of her reach and then howl hysterically as she tried in vain to reach them. He was surprised at the fight in the little thing. If he came near her, she would bite, spit and scratch like a wild animal. Just like her mother. Sometimes he made her sit with him on the worn out sofa and watch porn. He smoked incessantly and took pleasure in finding new places on her body to burn. The more she fought, the rougher he got.

Cigarette burns turned into rape, orally, vaginally and rectally. The child never quit fighting. As long as she was conscious, she was fighting. He enjoyed it quite a lot.

No one had been to visit him since the hospital. He had taken to delivering his goods or selling out of Joe's Booty Call. So, he was curious to see the dust kicking up on his driveway one afternoon. He could see the bubble lights on top and knew it was Travis Hampton, the police chief.

He didn't panic, but he did scramble to hide the girl.
It wouldn't do for Travis to find out about her. He
jerked her up from the floor. The girl began kicking and
screaming as usual. Earl wrapped his long, muscled
arms around her tiny body and covered her mouth with
his hand.

"You shut up, bitch, and be quiet or you'll pay
later," he growled in her ear.

Quickly grabbing the duct tape, he taped her wrists
and ankles and covered her mouth. Then he jerked open
the trap door in the floor and threw her in the root
cellar. He smoothed the tattered rag rug over the trap
door just as the chief was stepping out of his car. Earl
hobbled as fast as he could to meet Travis on the porch.

"Well, howdy, Chief," he drawled. "What brings
you to my neck of the woods?"

He didn't like Travis. Understandable since Earl
was on the wrong side of the law most of the time. But,
it was more than that. Travis had this holier-than-thou
attitude that just pissed him off. And he was smart. He
noticed the slightest thing out of place, the wrong look,
a nervous laugh. Anything would tip him off that
something wasn't kosher. And he was always right.
Travis' arrest record was better than any chief's had
been for twenty years. Earl avoided him at all costs.

But he couldn't avoid the man standing right in his damn yard!

"Hey, Earl," Travis replied. "There was a fire at the trailer park this mornin'. You hear about that?"

"Well, no, no I didn't," Earl said. "Know what happened?"

"Not yet. Seems as if the owner fell asleep with a lit cigarette," Travis said. "I'm askin' around tryin' to find out if she had any enemies or troubles."

"Well, chief, who has hurt?" Earl asked. "I been laid up, you know."

"It was old Faye. She didn't make it. No sign of Jody. No one's seen her in a couple of years. I know you hang out at the Booty Call where Jody worked. Any idea on where Jody is? I need to inform her of her mother's death."

Travis was staring hard at Earl. He knew about Earl's reputation with drugs and women. He had never been able to pin anything on him, though.

"No, Chief, they were just whores who provided a service," Earl said. "I heard they were hooked on the meth, but I don't know for sure. I've just been stayin' home tryin' to heal. Mindin' my own business. I ain't seen Faye for a couple of years, I would guess. You know, Jody talked about hitchin' a ride to Memphis a lot. Maybe someone over at the truck stop knows somethin'."

Earl fidgeted with his cigarette, trying to light it. This was not good. He had seen Faye at the Booty Call a couple weeks ago. She had looked bad. Hitting on every guy in the bar trying to get a fix. They just pushed her away and laughed. No one wanted anything, not even a blow job, from her anymore. Earl had reneged on his promise of free crystal, of course. After that first little bit, he had turned her away when she came begging. What was she gonna do? Call the police? She looked like a walking skeleton, skin stretched tight across her bones. Walking death, that's what she was. Walking death.

"Well, I'm just investigatin' to see if anythin' funny is goin' on," Travis said. "I might be needin' to interview you next week, if that's OK."

"Sure, Travis. Whatever you need, you just let me know," Earl chuckled. "I'll come to you next time."

Chief Travis started his car. "All right, Earl. You take care. I'll be in touch."

Earl relaxed a bit as the car backed away and drove off.

Well, hell. He'd have to be extra careful now. Didn't want ole Travis coming back, searching his property.

Travis had asked everyone he came across about Faye. Did she have enemies? Would she kill herself? Would someone kill her? If so, why? No one had answers. Most people either didn't remember her or didn't admit they remembered her. He found out she had been at the Booty Call recently, but there hadn't been any trouble.

He visited the trailer site and ruffled through the ashes. There was nothing of note that indicated foul play. The only strange thing he found was a baby diaper, cast out to the edges of the fire. He figured an onlooker must have dropped it. There was no reason for Faye to have baby diapers. No sign of Jody. Maybe she had gotten out after all. He wished her good luck. Anyplace was better than this for a girl like her.

A week later, Earl was slamming back whiskey shots at Joe's when Travis walked in the bar. Earl turned away, but Travis had already spotted him. Travis took the stool next to Earl's and ordered a beer.

"How's it goin', Earl," he asked.

"Oh, you know, just tryin' to get along," Earl responded.

"You know, Faye Collier's death has been ruled accidental, don't you?"

"No, I didn't, Travis. That's too bad. Cigarettes?"

"Yeah, she feel asleep, just like I thought. You know, I was lookin' at you for that fire," Travis said. He watched Earl's face. There was no hint of surprise.

"I didn't have anythin' to do with that, Travis! What do I have against Faye?" he said.

"Oh, I know you didn't have anything to do with it now, Earl. It's just that I figured Faye owed you money for somethin' and couldn't pay. That'd be a reason, wouldn't it?"

"Owe me money for what? I ain't got nothin' to sell her."

"Well, it's all water under the bridge right now, isn't it. I still haven't found Jody. Got any idea where she is?"

"Nope. And I'd appreciate it if you just leave me alone. I ain't done nothin' and I don't know nothin'. So just leave me alone."

Travis rose to leave. "I can't do that, Earl. I'll be watchin'."

Chapter 9

She didn't know his name. She didn't know her name, either. She had dreams sometimes in which she could hear someone whispering "my sweet Tess", over and over again. She didn't know who it was. She couldn't remember anyone ever being nice to her. But she always awoke feeling warm and happy. Of course, the instant she opened her eyes, she knew she was neither warm nor happy and she was certainly no one's "sweet Tess". She was in her room. Well, not really a room. It was a cellar of some sort with dirt floor and walls. The only items in the room were a makeshift bed and her food and water bowl pushed off into the corner of this tiny space. As usual, the bowls were empty. She would have to wait for the man to open the door at the top of her room and throw her some scraps from his supper. If he forgot, she'd have to make do with the insects that invaded her room from the earth around it. She had done it many times in her short life. She wanted to keep them as pets, something of her own. But the hunger took over and she always ended up eating them.

She was small for her age. The constant starvation and abuse had taken a toll on her small frame. She had been in the dirt room for as long as she could remember. Sometimes the man would let her out to "play". She always knew when it was playtime because she would get food that night. He would open the hatch and bark at her to climb up. Then he would make her take off her tattered clothing and douse her with a bucket of cold water. He said he couldn't bear her stink. He would plop her, naked, in a hard wooden chair at the table. Sometimes there would be a tiny pile of collard greens and a bit of pork fat on a plate in front of her. Occasionally, there would be a potato, but not often. He didn't want her getting fat. The first time, she had grabbed the plate and brought it to her face, slurping up the food as fast as she could. Suddenly, she felt a sharp pain on her hands and her plate fell to the floor spilling the food. The man had stabbed her hands with a fork.

"You eat when I tell you to eat," he roared, glaring at her with those dark, evil eyes. "Now get on the floor!

And don't get up until you have lapped up every bit of your mess!"

After eating, she would wait for him to give her the word. Sometimes, she sat for an hour, waiting. Sometimes, less, depending on his mood. After dinner, it was playtime. He had lots of games. If he was in a good mood, they would play Ride the Pony or Lick the Popsicle. Those were easy and didn't hurt her anymore. Mostly, he was in a bad mood, though, and then the games would hurt. A lot. There was Burn the Kitty, where he put cigarettes out on her girl parts. There was Hang Em High where he tied a noose around her neck and hung her from a coat hook for hours, toes barely touching the floor, while he bit her flesh and whipped her with a leather belt. And then there was The Tool Man. It was his favorite game. He used tools on this game. She fought him as hard as she could but it never helped. He seemed to enjoy her fighting him. If she passed out from the pain, he would wave some smelly stuff under her nose until she came to. After she was all bruised and bleeding and torn, he would jam his man part into her and start pumping wildly. At some point, he would moan and fall back. Then she knew it was over. She would be thrown back into her room until the next play time.

Despite the years of abuse, the girl did not lose her spirit. She fought him every time the door opened. She bit and kicked and screamed. She never made it easy for him. Something deep inside burned. She didn't know what it was, but it kept her going. At five years old, this was the only life she knew. Survival. She couldn't read or write. She had no way of knowing how the world outside worked other than what she saw on television. But she knew she hated the man and this place.

It was always dark in her room. The batteries in the flashlight had died long ago. If the man forgot to cover the trap door, light would filter in from above. She developed a keen sense of hearing being in the dark all the time. She could hear the television and radio when he was home. She heard noises outside. People talking to the man. She heard the little critters scurrying in the dirt of her room.

Time passed slowly between play dates with the man. She would draw crude pictures on her walls and floor. Flowers and such. She could look at the pictures and imagine a happy place. A house, sunshine, puppy, flowers. Anything that kept her mind off the horror she lived in now. The pictures kept her spirit up. She also had a crudely made rag doll who was her only friend. She would talk to her about all her wishes. She didn't dwell on the pain. There was no help for that. But if she focused on the life she wanted, things didn't seem so bad. The doll helped her do that.

Most of the time she slept. She couldn't tell if it was day or night because her biorhythm was all messed up. Sometimes she stretched and jumped just to keep the boredom away. Her little 5-year-old mind didn't know all of this was preparing her for the next fight.

Every two or three days, the man would throw a bottle of water and some food down. She had learned to ration the water and save the food for the times he was gone for several days at a time. That didn't happen too often anymore. Something had happened a long time ago that had hurt him. He had started staying around the house longer and longer periods until soon he didn't leave at all. He would leave in the evening sometimes and come home smelling real bad. Those nights, he stumbled and cursed and usually slept on the floor. But at least he left her alone those nights.

Until the night he didn't. She could hear him stumbling around upstairs, knocking around furniture as he made his way across the room. She thought, well, I'm safe tonight. Suddenly, the hatch flew open and there he was. Weaving around at the top with the light to his back, he looked like a dark, hairy shadow monster.

He growled, "Come on, little girl. Time to play!"

Wearily, she climbed up the ladder. He had pulled his pants down and was sitting on the kitchen chair, staring at her drunkenly, bottle in hand. He grabbed her by the hair and shoved her face in his crotch. She knew what to do.

When he finished, he lay his head on the table and began snoring. She couldn't believe it! He was so drunk he had forgotten to lock her up! She grabbed his shirt from the floor and quietly inched over to the door, stopping every time the floor creaked. The screen door squeaked as she carefully opened it. Still he didn't move. She made her way off the porch and ran.

She ran like a wild thing was chasing her. She knew she had to get as far away as possible before he came to and realized she was missing. She turned towards the woods.

The thorns ripped her tender flesh leaving streaks of blood running down her face and arms. After a while, Tess crouched in the tangled patch of thorns and briars, shaking. It was so dark, especially this deep in the woods. The moon's light couldn't penetrate the dense canopy of trees and kudzu. She listened intently. She heard the hoot of an owl on her left and a responding hoot on her right. The coyotes were yipping at a distance. A garter snake slithered across her feet. She

didn't hear the man. She had run until she couldn't see
the house anymore. And then she ran some more. Now
she was tired. Her dirty blond hair hadn't been cleaned
in a long time and was now a matted, muddy mess. It
blended perfectly with the scraggly thorn bushes around
her. Her survival instincts had been honed over the last
few years. She knew she had to stay quiet. And small.
Maybe she could make it till morning. She crouched a
little lower.

Located alongside a narrow gravel road in Bolivar
County, the woods were overgrown and hard to
traverse. Especially at night. Mosquitoes, katydids and
an occasional owl filled the air with noises that terrified
young and old alike. No one ever visited these woods in
the day, much less at night. The thorns and vines were
so tangled that only wild creatures could get through.
Wild creatures like fox, snakes, spiders, coons and
coyotes. And the man. He seemed to be able to walk
through this awful place with ease. She thought it was
because he was so evil that everything in nature shrank
with fear and let him pass. She just hoped he would
have trouble tonight. Just long enough for her to rest.
She snuggled deeper into her little nest and fell
sound asleep.

There's no such thing as luck, he thought as he
perused the selection of candies and goodies in the 7-

11. There were only choices. And mistakes. He had made a mistake and now the little twit was loose. He picked up the moon pie. Chocolate or banana? It felt like a chocolate day, dark and moody and delicious.

The fashion Barbie at the register gave him a warm, inviting smile as he made his way to the front. She had seen him come in and instantly turned on the charm. She pushed her long auburn hair behind her ear and winked at him. Her hazel eyes watched as he moved through the store. She licked her lips sensually as he made his way up front. His dark hair and eyes gave him that smoldering look that the ladies loved. His 6'4" body was sinewy and lean. At first glance, people usually compared him to a young Elvis. Upon closer inspection, though, his eyes were black and menacing. His crooked smile was hard and insincere. When Barbie's eyes met his, she felt a shiver of fear. Her sensual smile faded quickly. A shiver ran through her. Suddenly, she couldn't wait for him to leave. He chuckled. He payed for his moon pie and his RC Cola and ambled out of the store.

Mississippi is hot at night. And humid. The mosquitoes were already attacking him. That was OK. He liked the tiny little pricks of pain. He rubbed the cold, icy can of RC Cola along his forehead. She was going to pay for this little escapade. He smiled at the thought. Oh, yes, she was definitely going to pay.

He had been foolish enough, not to mention drunk, and had forgotten to lock her back up. When he awoke a half hour later, the little twit was gone.

He knew she was in the woods. It was the logical place for a child to hide. The nearest neighbor was three miles down the road. All the neighbors on his road were meth addicts and would bring her back to him in hopes of a reward. There was no way she could make three miles, if she even knew about it. No, the woods was where she would run.

Chapter 10

It was dawn when Tess awoke. At first, she didn't remember. She suddenly became alert, looking for any sign of danger. It was a miracle that he hadn't found her. She knew he liked to hunt and was surprised he hadn't been able to follow her trail. She had been careful, though, stepping on rocks and fallen limbs instead of the ground. And there were no paths in these woods, just tangled webs of branches and vines. So, she had gotten lucky. So far, so good.

She had unknowingly fallen asleep in a patch of raspberry vines. It was mid summer and the juicy, deep purple berries were all around. There hadn't been time for the birds to get them yet. Breakfast was good. She ate as many as she could find. Her little hands and face was sticky with raspberry juice. After breakfast, she had to decide how to get out. She was too short to get a long view of her location. She had no idea where the nearest help was. She needed to know which way to go.

The trees were all covered in kudzu. Kudzu is a climbing, coiling and trailing perennial vine. It's another one of those invasive species from Asia that spreads like wildfire. It climbs over trees and grows so rapidly that it kills the trees by shielding them from the sun. It is also strong and used in fiber arts, such as basketry and paper making, and, hopefully, climbing.

Tess cautiously tested the vine by putting her entire weight on it. It held. She climbed a foot or so higher. It still held. Soon she had climbed twenty feet and still it held. She kept climbing until she got to the first limb. As she rested on the limb, she looked out over the woods.

To the east, as far as she could see there were trees. She turned to the west. The woods continued for as far as she could see here, too, but there seemed to be a break in the trees. It looked like the woods were divided. By what, she didn't know, but that seemed like a sign to go that way.

Suddenly, she heard a loud noise. A second later, something slammed into the tree above her head. She frantically climbed back down the tree and began making her way through the vines. It didn't occur to her that someone had shot at her.

Earl did, indeed, like to hunt. Not necessarily for food. He always tried to shoot to wound the animal. Then he would move up close to watch it slowly die. There was something godly about watching the life ebb from a living thing. Most of the time, he would leave it lie, wasting the meat.

Like any good hunter, he got into his tree stand in the east woods well before dawn. He was dressed in camouflage and face paint. No one would be able to spot him even if they were looking. And from his perch, he could see any movement for at least a mile in any direction.

He saw the little brat climbing up the tree through the scope on his rifle. She was at least a mile and a half to the west of him. That didn't bother him. He knew these woods and could cover that distance in a short time. He'd be on her before she could get too far. He squeezed the trigger, aiming just above her head, and watched as she hurried back down the tree and headed for the highway that divided the woods. He had missed her on purpose. Just wanted to scare her a little. He chuckled as he climbed out of the tree stand and headed west. It was slow going for most people because of the brush and thorns, but he had learned how to move through them easily long ago. He figured he'd catch her before the hour was up.

Earl moved fast. He had lost sight of the girl, but he knew she was headed for the highway. If she stayed in a straight line from the tree to the highway, he would catch her. The little brat was leaving almost no tracks to follow. She was so small, her footprints did not leave marks on the ground cover. Nor were there any broken limbs. If he hadn't seen her from his tree stand, he would never have known where she was.

His hunting instincts told him he was close to his prey. The little hairs on the back of his neck stood up. He stood still, sniffing the air, listening. He slowly began moving again, quietly padding on the ground. He had tracked prey many times and was usually successful. Tracking a little girl shouldn't be a problem.

Tess had found that running through the woods was not possible. She had to pick her way through the thorny brush step by step. Her little arms and legs were covered in scratches from the thorns, and mosquitoes were in a feeding frenzy on her blood.

She couldn't feel the bites, though. Her only thought was getting away. She had that primal instinct of survival. If the man caught her, he would kill her. Of that, she was sure.

So far she had been lucky. He had not come after her. Or at least, she didn't know if he had or not. Surely she would have heard him. He was a lot bigger than she was so she knew he would make a lot of noise coming through the woods. She had not associated the loud noise in the tree with the man.

She trudged along for while before stumbling over a tree root. She fell face first into the brush. More scratches. She was so tired. She need to rest. There were fallen trees all around, covered in kudzu. One had fallen and lay a little off to the side. She thought she could hide behind it and rest a bit. When she got around to the other side of the tree, she discovered it was just a shell of an ash tree. The inside had rotted out and the space was just big enough to for her to fit. She pulled aside the vines, crawled in and replaced the vines. It was so cozy, she drifted off the sleep in no time.

She was awoken by the snap of a twig. Her eyes flew open. She held her breath. He was standing just outside of her hideaway!

The man stood there a moment. She heard him sniff like he had a runny nose. He turned and looked all around. So far, he had his back to the hollowed out tree and hadn't noticed it. He appeared to be scanning the entire forest floor looking for her. He sat down on the tree, so close she could have reached out and touched his leg. A spider crawled over her face. She didn't move. After a moment, the man moved on. Still quiet, still searching.

Tess propped herself up on her elbow. She was terrified. What was she to do now? She couldn't continue the direction she had been going because the man was going that way. She couldn't go back. Never. She decided to wait until nightfall. Maybe it would be safe by then. She lay back down, but this time, she did not fall asleep. The man was near and she had to be vigilant.

Earl reached the highway about a half hour later. It was clear. There was no sign of the child. Damn it! Where could she be? He was sure he had been close. Had she changed directions? He didn't think so. The only answer was that she had beaten him to the highway and been picked up. He looked around for the police. If she had been found, Travis would be here soon investigating. He did not want to be around when that happened. He turned and headed back into the woods. He wasn't as quiet this time. He wanted to be home if Travis came knocking at this door.

Tess heard him tromping through the woods like a bull moose. Obviously, he wasn't being cautious. Did that mean he had quit looking for her? She couldn't be sure, so she waited until she could no longer hear him.

She slowly moved the vines from the opening and crawled out. She looked all around. There was no sign of him. What had happened? She didn't believe he had given up. But something had spooked him and he had turned for home. Relief swept through her tiny frame.

There was still some daylight left as Tess headed toward the highway again. The going was easier now since the man had crashed through the brush. She just followed his path and soon came upon the highway. She stood there, looking in both directions, unsure of which way would lead her away from hell.

Chapter 11

Coop had been into Gnaw Bone for his weekly grocery run. He shopped at Wal-Mart because the prices were lower and he only had his social security check to live on. His truck was a 64 Ford F-150. It used to be green and white, but now it was more like rust and more rust. It rattled and shook until he felt his false teeth would fall out. But he loved it. As long as it was running, he would keep it.

It was almost dark. He reached down to pull the lights on. When he looked up, he slammed on the brakes and turned the steering wheel. The truck ground to a screeching halt. There in the road was a small child. Looked like a girl, but could have been a boy. He couldn't tell. The child was filthy. It had blood all over its arms and legs. The hair was caked with mud and twigs. It was wearing an oversized tattered shirt and, apparently, nothing else.

Coop was 80 years old and thought he had seen everything. He had never seen anything like this. Why was this little thing out here all alone on the road at night? He slowly walked over to the child, careful not to move too fast for fear of scaring it. He could see it was a girl, now. Her features were too fine to be male. He slowly reached his hand toward her and she shrank away.

He said, "Here, here, girly. I ain't gonna hurt you."

She stood still, staring at him.

He reached into his pocket and pulled out a peppermint. He carried them all the time. It was his favorite candy.

Still cautious, she trembled as she reached out and took the candy. She ripped the plastic off and crammed it into her mouth. Poor child was starving! he thought. He pulled out another one and held it out.

After the third mint, the child inched closer to him, looking at his pocket. He turned and hobbled over to the passenger door and opened it. The girl didn't move. He held up the candy and gestured to the door. She came closer. He laid the candy on the seat and walked around to the driver's side. She was still standing motionless when he slid into the seat. He sat there and waited for her. After a few minutes, she slowly moved toward the passenger side. She peeked around the door at him. He sat very still and didn't look at her. She could see the candy on the seat, but she couldn't reach it without getting up into the truck.

She climbed up into the truck, snatched the peppermint and jumped back down. She obviously didn't trust him, but he knew she needed help.

He took the bag of mints out of the console and lay it on the seat next to him.

She climbed back into the truck and reached for the bag. He gently placed his hand over it, so she couldn't get it. She gave him a look that broke his heart. He motioned for her to sit on the passenger side. Slowly she sat down, never taking her eyes off of him. He handed her a mint. She took the mint, but kept her eyes on him and the bag.

He took the bag and climbed out of the truck. He slowly walked around the truck and handed her another mint as he closed the passenger door. She sat very still, watching. When he got back in the driver's seat, he gave her the entire bag and started down the road.

Coop drove as fast has his old truck would allow back into Gnaw Bone, straight to the police station.

Travis' car was sitting out front when he pulled up. He turned to the child.

"I'll be right back," he said, gently. "You stay here and eat your candy."

She just stared at him. But she gave no sign of jumping out.

Chapter 12

Travis had been chief of police for twelve years now. He preferred the small town office to the Jackson office he had been at the previous ten years. The slow pace suited him. He knew most of the people in town and around the outskirts. He knew who was trouble and who was not. There were rarely any surprises here in Gnaw Bone. Until now.

Coop burst through his door like a bat out of hell. He was gasping for breath and motioning outside.

"Travis!" he croaked. "You have to come!"

Travis hurried over to catch him before he fell. Coop was a upstanding citizen, but he was on in years and appeared to be quite fragile.

"What on earth, Coop?" he said. "Sit down."

"No, Travis! She was in the woods over by the highway! Help her!"

Travis looked out at the truck. He could barely make out someone sitting in the passenger seat. He sat Coop down on the bench and went outside. He stood there for a second gauging the situation. Was that a dog? he thought. He knew Coop had a mangy old mutt, but he had never known him to take the dog in the truck.

He walked over to the passenger side and peeked in the window. Staring back at him was a set of sad, bright blue eyes. It was a child! She was holding a bag of peppermints in her small dirty hands. He couldn't tell the color of her hair because it was caked with mud and twigs as if it had never been washed. She had on a tattered work shirt from the cotton mill that pretty much swallowed up her whole little body. Her exposed skin was covered in scratches and dried blood. She had no shoes.

"Be gentle, Travis," Coop yelled. "She scares easy."

Travis slowly opened the door and squatted so he was eye level with her. She stared at him, never moving. Alert. Wary.

"Hey, sweetie," Travis said in a low voice. "What's your name?"

His voice sounded gravelly and familiar, as if she had heard him before. His eyes were warm, full of concern.

"Tess," she whispered. She had dreamt it, but it seemed as good a name as any.

"Hey, Tess. My name is Travis," he said. "Can you tell me where you live?"

She shook her head. If she told him she lived in the shack, he might make her go back. He might even be friends with the man. Suddenly, she was frightened. She shrank away from Travis and scooted to the middle of the seat.

"Hey, hey, wait a minute," Travis said softly. "It's okay. There's no need to be afraid. Do you want somethin' to eat?"

She nodded vigorously and he held out his arms.

"Come on then. We'll get you inside and get somethin' to eat," he said as he lifted her out of the truck. She weighed next to nothing.

He took her inside the office and sat her on the bench. He fetched her some water from the cooler. She gulped it down and held her cup out for more. Poor thing was dehydrated! How long had she been in the woods?

He called Sue over at the diner and asked her to have some chicken and dumplings delivered to the office. And some chocolate milk. His next call was to Dr. Beth Rhodes. He told her the situation and asked her to come by as soon as she could. She said she would be right over.

Travis sat down next to Tess on the bench.

"Tess," he said. "Why were you in the woods? Did somethin' scare you?"

She nodded ever so slightly.

"Okay. What scared you?"

She didn't answer.

"Do you know your mommy or daddy's name?"

"I don't have one," she whispered, shaking her head.

"Well, where do you live?"

"In my room."

"And where is your room?" Travis asked.

"I don't know," she answered.

Tess lay her head on his shoulder. She liked him. He wasn't mean to her.

Travis met Sue at the door when she knocked. He wanted as few people as possible to know about Tess until he figured out what was going on, and Sue was the town gossip.

"Chocolate milk, Travis," Sue chuckled. "Don't tell me you're goin' all soft on me!"

"No," he replied. "Just a little stomach trouble, Sue. Thanks for deliverin'. I appreciate it."

"No worries. Let me know if you need anythin' else," she said over her shoulder as she turned and headed back to the diner.

He opened the tray of food and handed it to Tess. The aroma made his mouth water. Sue's chicken and dumplings was the best in the county. Suddenly, he wished he had ordered enough for himself.

Tess put her face in the tray and began slurping at the food, like a dog. Travis gently took her head in his hands and raised it up. He wiped her face with the napkin Sue had included. He put the fork in her hands and showed her how to use it. It took her a couple of tries before she got the hang of it. Then she started wolfing it down.

Travis was confused. How could a five-year-old not know how to use a fork? Where had she come from? It was as if she were a feral animal. The knock on the door startled him from his thoughts. He peeked out the window to see a stunning woman with brunette hair and an infectious smile. Dr. Beth Rhodes just happened to be the only doctor in town and his fiancé. He opened the door and ushered her in, closing the door quickly.

"Travis, what on earth?"she gasped when she saw Tess. "Who is this poor thing?"

"I don't know," he said, "but she needs your help."

"Oh, you poor darlin'," Beth whispered to Tess.

She knelt down next to Tess and looked her over. Tess stared right back. She had never seen a woman before except on television. The only real person she knew was the man. And now Travis, the old man with peppermint and this woman.

"My name is Beth," Beth said. "Is it OK if I clean you up?"

Tess didn't know what that meant but she figured if Travis liked this woman, she should, too. She nodded.

Beth took her hand and led Tess into the back of the police station. She opened a door which led into Travis's lodging. The job didn't pay much, but it did include a one bedroom apartment in the back of the station.

Tess looked around the apartment while Beth ran a bath. She had never been in such a luxurious place before. There were curtains, a nice couch, shelves of books and albums, pictures on the wall. Travis must be rich to have so much! She walked over to the bathroom door.

The steam was rising from a big white bowl thing. Beth added something to the water and suddenly there were suds everywhere. Tess giggled. Beth turned around and motioned for her to come over.

Tess couldn't keep her eyes off the mounds of suds in the bowl. Were they soft? Wet? They looked like clouds. While she was watching the suds, Beth pulled the shirt over Tess' head and gasped.

The child had scars and marks all over her body, not just the scratches and blood she had seen earlier. This girl was a victim of long term abuse even a grown woman would have trouble surviving. She instinctually grabbed Tess and hugged her close. She felt tears well in her eyes and hurriedly wiped them away before Tess saw.

"Come on, Tess," she said. "Let's get in the tub."

She helped Tess climb in the tub. The water enveloped her up to her shoulders. She saw fear in Tess' eyes.

"It's okay, Tess," she laughed. "It's just water."

She began to gently wash her with a soft cloth. The dirt and blood washed away to reveal beautifully soft, white skin. The only blemishes were the scars and scratches. She had Tess lean her head back as she washed the crud from her hair, revealing thick, gleaming blonde hair underneath all the dirt. She let Tess play until the water turned cold and the suds were gone. Tess didn't seem to mind the cold water.

Tess had never had a bath before that she could remember. There was nothing like this in the man's house. But she loved it. The water was so warm and silky.

She gently lifted Tess from the water and wrapped a big, fluffy towel around her. Her body was so thin, the towel wrapped around her twice. After she dried her off, Beth took some lotion in her hand and smoothed it all over Tess' skin. While Tess sat on the bed in the towel, Beth brushed her tangled hair until it was smooth as silk. She then took a clean white t-shirt from Travis' drawers and pulled it over Tess' head. Tess was fading fast. The food and warm bath had relaxed her so much she could hardly hold her eyes open. Beth tucked her under the covers, kissed her forehead and turned out the light. She expected Tess to complain about the darkness, but she heard not a word. Tess was already asleep.

Beth softly closed the bedroom door. Travis was sitting on the sofa.

"How's she doin'?" he asked.

Beth sighed as she sat next to him.

"Her body's in bad shape," she said. "But her psyche is remarkably good. She's got all these old and new scars all over her body. It's as if she doesn't notice them."

Travis put his arm around her, and she lay her head on his shoulder.

"Did she tell you who her parents are or where she lives?"

"She said she doesn't have any. What does that mean, Travis? Why was she in the woods?" she asked.

"I don't know, but I'm gonna to find out. Tomorrow," he whispered. "Do you want to stay here tonight? I'll pull out the sofa bed."

"I think I will," she said. "I want to be here if she wakes up."

Chapter 13

Travis rolled out of bed before dawn the next morning. He left Beth snuggled in the blankets sound asleep while he made coffee. He tiptoed to the bedroom door and peeked in. He couldn't see Tess in the darkened room, but he saw the small bump under the covers move when the door creaked. He closed the door and went back to the kitchen.

He poured his coffee into a tall mug and left the apartment. The office was empty. The town could only afford one law enforcement officer. That was him. The most popular crime in the town was drug dealing. Other crimes were petty thievery, drunken brawls and, every once in a while, prostitution. All drug crime offenders he would transport to the county seat for incarceration and trial. The others would stay overnight in one of the two cells in the office until they sobered up or confessed to the thievery. The drunks and hookers got to go home; the thieves would agree to apologize and reimburse the victim or do community service. There was no need to involve courts most of the time. That's how small town justice worked.

But, this. He had never seen anything like this even during his time on the Jackson police force nor during his military service as an Army Ranger. Someone knew something about this little girl.

Travis left the office and headed for Coop's house. He knew Coop was an early riser. He wasn't surprised that Coop opened the door before he had a chance to knock.

"How's the little girl doin', Travis?" Coop said. "I prayed for her last night."

"She's restin' now, Coop. I know it's early, but would you show me where you picked her up?" Travis asked.

"Sure thing. Let me get my hat."

On the way to the woods, Coop couldn't stop talking. He asked Travis all kinds of questions about the girl. Who was she? Where did she come from? What happened to her? Travis couldn't answer any of them. Eventually, they rode in silence.

Coop pointed to the spot on the side of the road where the little girl had been standing. Travis pulled over.

He got out and surveyed the area. There was nothing unusual. The trees and brush were covered with kudzu like all the woods in the area. The noxious weed had been introduced into the area long ago for erosion control. It had rapidly become invasive and dangerous to the native woods. Now every tree and shrub was covered in it.

He noticed a disturbance in the wall of kudzu. This must be where she had emerged from the woods. He stepped over to the gap and peeked inside the woods. He could see a trail where the ground had been flattened by someone walking. But the trail was too wide to have been made by a tiny thing like Tess. Someone must have been chasing her.

He dropped Coop off at his house and headed back to Gnaw Bone. The town was just waking up. Sue's diner had opened and the place was hopping. It was a regular gathering place for all the old codgers in town. They would tell stories of their glory days and discuss all the rumors Sue had let them in on. He pulled into the parking lot and entered the diner. Several patrons called out "Hey, want some chocolate milk, killer?" and laughed. Travis laughed, too, and waved them off. It was all in good fun.

"Mornin', Travis!" Sue called out from behind the counter. "You want your regular?"

"Yeah, but make it a triple," Travis said. "Beth is at my place and you know how she can eat!"

As he waited on his order, he listened to the small talk going on around him. There was talk about the latest tractor someone had bought, the newcomers moving into the new subdivision, the school play coming up. But there was nothing about a little girl who lived in the woods.

Sue gave him his order and he waved as he left, leaving behind calls of "Bye, chocolate milk!"

Travis opened the door to his office and stopped in his tracks. There was the most beautiful little girl in the middle of the floor playing with dolls. She had gorgeous blonde hair, pulled up in a pony tail with a little pink ribbon. She was wearing a lacy, flouncy pink dress which spread all around her as she sat on the floor. Shiny white shoes and frilly pink socks adorned her feet. Never had he seen a child so precious.

Beth walked over to him and took the food. She whispered, "I had Billy from the mercantile bring over some things for her. Told him I needed them for one of my patients. He didn't see her."

"She's the spittin' image of someone," he said. "I just can't place her."

Beth took the food into the apartment and began setting the table. She had decided that the sooner Tess became acclimated to normal life rather than the hell she had been living, the better off she would be. Travis didn't have much in the way of niceties. He was a typical bachelor. But she had found an old tablecloth in the closet and spread it over the worn dining room table. She placed three plates, glasses and silverware. She opened the food boxes and distributed the food to each place setting. She poured herself and Travis some coffee and Tess some chocolate milk.

She stepped back into the office to announce breakfast and was immediately body slammed by a little girl dressed in pink. Tess wrapped her tiny arms around Beth's legs and hugged her tightly.

Beth pried her loose and knelt down. Tess looked at her with her eyes filled with tears.

"Thank you," she stammered. "For my things. I love them."

Beth hugged her back, holding her tightly.

"You are most welcome, sweetheart," she whispered. "Now, come eat."

Beth sat next to Tess and showed her how to use her napkin to keep her dress clean. She showed her how to

use a knife and fork to cut her food into small bites.
Beth took her own chair and began eating, keeping an
eye on Tess. Tess struggled with the concept of
utensils, but she had managed to keep the food on the
fork and get it to her mouth. Beth beamed at Travis.

While Beth cleared the table, Travis took Tess'
hand and led her to the couch. When he tried to sit next
to her, she got a frightened look on her face and moved
away. He had no way of knowing this was a situation
she was quite familiar with. Eat, sit on the couch,
and pain.

When he saw her fear, he pulled a chair over and sat
directly across from her. He could see the fear fade
from her face. He leaned over and clasped his hands
so she could see he was no threat. She looked at
him warily.

"Tess," he said. "I need to talk about what happened
to you. I need to know who hurt you."

Tess looked down at her doll. He could barely hear
her when she whispered, "The man."

"Do you know his name?" he asked.

"No." Still looking down.

"Do you know where he lives?"

"In the woods."

"How long were you with him?"

"Always."

"Where's your mama?"

"I don't have one," she sobbed.

"Okay, okay," he said. "It's okay. Can you tell me what the man looks like?"

"Big. And mean."

"What else? What color is his hair? His eyes?"

She thought for a minute. "Dark," she answered. "Like yours."

That hit him like a brick. No wonder she was wary with him. He reminded her of the monster that had kept her. He would have to keep reminding himself to be gentle with her.

"Oh, sweetie, I'm sorry," he whispered. "I will never hurt you. I'm gonna to help you, okay?"

Tess nodded.

Travis stood up and looked at Beth.

"Can you stay with her today? I know your schedule is busy, but I want to keep her out of sight until I know what's goin' on. Will you..."

Beth had crossed the room and put her fingers on his lips.

"Of course, I will. I have a light day today and I can reschedule all of them. In fact, I'll take the week off. I need to know what happened too," she said.

Knowing that Tess was well tended, Travis decided to check out the woods where she was found. He drove out to where Coop had shown him. He parked the patrol truck on the side of the road. He took water, a flashlight, and his weapon and headed down the recently made trail. As he walked slowly along the trail, he looked for any clue. Cigarette butts, candy wrappers, pop bottles. Anything that might have DNA or give a clue as to who had smashed this path. There was nothing. He did find a tree about a half mile in that had fallen. The inside had been eaten away. The only reason it caught his attention was that the mass of kudzu that covered the tree had been disturbed. As if something had taken shelter inside the tree.

He followed the trail quite a while until it ended at County Road 1100. Several people lived along this five-mile dirt road. Mostly poor people who lived off government handouts. Their homes were barely livable shacks that had little insulation and leaky roofs. Travis knew that several of these people cooked meth, but mostly for their own use. The only one he suspected of selling was Earl Fields. His place was all the way down at the end of the road.

Travis decided to start interviewing the folks in the area first thing in the morning. By the time he hiked his way back to his truck, it would be late afternoon. He wanted to talk to Tess some more about the man she was so afraid of.

Beth had spent the day putting Tess at ease. The child had warmed to her quickly and rarely left her side all day. They had swept the floors, made the bed, washed the dishes. Tess did well with those chores, which made Beth think that she had done them before.

She had not asked Tess any questions all day. She wanted to provide a safe, loving environment and did not want to stress her out by asking her to confront her past. At least not right now. Travis could do that. Tess needed someone to whom she could turn without fearing an inquisition.

Travis brought home supper again and they all sat at the table and ate. Tess was better with the utensils this meal, although she was still a little awkward. Beth and Travis carried on small talk while they ate. Tess concentrated on managing the fork and food. Every once in a while, she would look up as if interested in what the adults were saying.

When they were done eating, Beth took Tess aside. She knelt down and looked her in the eyes.

"Tess," she said softly. "I need to leave for a while to get some clothes and check in on my office. Will you be okay stayin' with Travis while I'm gone?"

Tess looked at Travis guardedly. Beth could see the uncertainty on her face.

"Sweetie, Travis is a good man. He will keep you safe. You don't need to be afraid of him. He will take care of you. I promise," said Beth.

"Okay, Beth," she whispered. "But you'll come back soon?"

"Sure, honey, as quickly as I can," Beth reassured her.

After Beth left, Travis asked Tess to sit on the couch. He took the chair opposite.

"Tess," he said. " I don't want you to be afraid of me. I won't hurt you. I just want to find out what happened to you so I can keep it from happenin' to some other little girl. Understand?"

Tess nodded her head.

"Do you think you can talk to me about what happened to you?" he asked.

Tess thought a moment and then nodded again.

"Let's start with where you lived. Can you tell me what it looked like?"

Tess hesitated, thinking.

"There was a table and a couch. He had a TV," Tess said.

"Hmm. What did your room look like?" Travis asked.

"It was under the floor," said Tess. "It had dirt walls and was dark all the time."

"What did you sleep on?"

"I had an old blanket."

"What did you eat?"

"The man threw food down sometimes. I don't know what it was. I ate the bugs when he forgot," Tess whispered. "He forgot a lot."

Travis felt a lump rise in his throat. He cleared his throat before speaking.

"Tess, this is a hard question and I hope you can answer it for me because it is very important."

Tess finally looked up and stared at him.

"How did you get all those marks on your body," he asked gently.

Tears welled in her eyes. She took a moment to answer. When she did, her voice was shaky and very low. He had to strain to hear her. She told him every detail of what the man had done to her for as long as she could remember. She described sitting on the torn, blue couch and watching porn, getting burned by cigarettes. She pointed to the scars and described the tool that had been used. She didn't know the tool names, but she definitely remembered every detail of them. When she finished, she was sobbing. She looked up at Travis and saw that he, too, had tears on his cheek. She took her small hand and lay it on his cheek, wiping the tears away. He started sobbing and held her tightly in his arms while they both cried.

Travis composed himself and wiped Tess' face with a tissue. She was sitting in his lap. She no longer seemed afraid of him.

"Tess," he said. "I promise nothin' like that will ever happen to you again. I am gonna to find this man and put him in jail. He will never hurt you again. Do you believe me?"

Tess nodded. She believed everything he said. She felt a huge weight had been lifted from her shoulders. She felt safe.

Tess was in bed when Beth returned. She tiptoed into the bedroom and gave Tess a kiss on the forehead.

"You came back," Tess said sleepily.

Beth smiled. "I told you I would. Good night, sweetheart."

Beth fell on the couch next to Travis. He was uncharacteristically somber. Beth could tell he had been crying.

"Did you get what you needed from her," she asked quietly.

He nodded. They sat in silence for a while. Travis told her he would have to call the county social worker tomorrow to tell her about Tess but he was afraid they would take her away. Beth sat straight up.

"You can not send her to a foster home, Travis!" she declared. "You will not!"

"I have to, Beth. It's the law," he replied.

"No! She's still in danger! We have to find out who did this first!" she begged.

Travis shook his head. He didn't want to let go of Tess yet. He needed her to identify the pervert who had hurt her. And he needed to find her parents.

"Okay," he said, wearily. "We'll keep her here under wraps for a little while longer. But, you know, I'm gonna to have to call county eventually."

Beth lay her head on Travis' shoulder. They both silently pondered what lay ahead for little Tess. Neither could imagine a good outcome.

They fell asleep in each other's arms on the sofa bed. Both sensed that life was about to change.

Chapter 14

Earl had seen Travis tromping through the woods. He had been sitting in his tree stand, hoping to catch sight of the little twit. But, instead, he saw Travis following the crude path he himself had made last night. He had been so stupid! He should have known she had gotten away and covered his tracks! Now it was no longer something between he and the girl. Now Travis was involved.

Earl waited until Travis turned to return to his truck before climbing out of the tree stand. He had work to do.

He rushed to his cabin and began erasing any sign of the child. He gathered up his playthings and what few toys the girl had had.

He cleared everything from the cellar where she had stayed. He threw out the milk in the refrigerator. He piled all the stuff in the center of a blanket and bundled it up.

The land around Earl's house was full of forest, gullies and ravines. The ground was hard. Too difficult to dig by hand. The forest was hard for men to traverse, but a tracking dog could get through it with no problem. So that ruled out hiding the stuff in the woods or burying it in the ground. His only option was to trek it far into the hillside and hide it in a gully.

Earl hiked for two hours before he came to a place he thought was safe. There were natural cave formations in the rocky hillside. They weren't deep caves, but deep enough to hold the bundle. The one he chose was concealed by scraggly brush at the opening. He carefully placed the bundle inside and rearranged the brush so no one could spot the disturbance. He returned to the cabin, retracing his steps and erasing his trail as he went.

Once in the cabin, he scoured the cabin all over again to be sure he hadn't missed something. Satisfied there was no sign of the girl, he sat down and drank until he passed out on the floor.

Chapter 15

Travis had breakfast with Beth and Tess. It was a beautiful, sunshiny morning. It was only eight o'clock and already the temperature had hit ninety degrees. Today was going to be a scorcher. Travis grabbed his coffee and a thermos of water and headed out to do his interviews.

When he reached the first house, actually a mobile trailer, on County Road 1100, he just sat for a moment and surveyed the property. This was the home of Steve "Red" Mills. He knew for a fact that Red cooked meth because he had caught him in the act several years ago. But Red didn't sell. No one knew how old he was but Travis suspected at least 70. It's hard to tell with meth addicts. The drug ages users so fast, they can be 30 but look 70. They usually have stained, broken and rotted teeth. They scratch and pick at their skin as if insects were crawling inside of them. Their bodies are extremely thin due to loss of appetite and they exhibit jerky, erratic twitching. But the particular symptom Travis was worried about at the moment was paranoia. Meth users are always paranoid, thinking people are out to steal their possessions. This paranoia makes them dangerous. Especially to a cop showing up in the driveway early in the morning.

So Travis took a moment to put on his Kevlar vest, check his spare magazine of ammo, and unfasten his holster.

He got out and stood behind his door.

"Red!" he yelled. "This is the police. I just want to talk to you."

No sign of movement inside the shack.

"Red! Come on out, Red. You're not in trouble. I just wanna talk!" he yelled again.

He saw movement at the front window. The curtains had fluttered just a moment. A second later he saw the front door crack open and he put his hand on his weapon. Now who's paranoid, he thought.

A skeleton stepped out. The man was so skinny, Travis could see nearly every bone. Red had picked his hair out so that now there were only small patches of what used to be red hair on his head. He was unwashed, unshaven and shirtless, wearing bib overalls that hung from his thin frame. His dull skin had a yellow tinge to it that signaled liver failure. He was also holding a shotgun down by his side.

"What you want, Chief?" he asked in a raspy voice.

"Put your gun down, Red," he replied. "I just want to talk. Okay if I come on up?"

Red put his shotgun back inside the door and motioned for Travis to come. With his hand still on his weapon, Travis walked up to the steps.

"Hey, Red. How ya doin'," he asked, lapsing into country slang.

"Oh, ya know. Just tryin' to get by," Red replied with chuckle and then a cough.

Travis said, "I'm wonderin' if you've seen anyone around here with a little girl, bout five years old. You mighta seen her wanderin' on the road."

Red shook his head. "Naw, ain't no kids on this road. I'm sorry for 'em if they live around here. This ain't no place for kids, for sure," he said as he scratched his arm.

"Are you sure, Red," Travis insisted. "Cause I know there was a little girl somewhere on this road. You sure?"

Red nodded, looking down at his feet. He didn't want no trouble with the law. He liked Travis cause he left him alone, even though he knew he cooked meth. So he wanted no trouble.

"I'm sure, Chief. Ain't been no kids of any kind around here."

Travis nodded and turned to go.

"Well, thanks anyway, Red. You let me know if you hear anything, okay."

"Yes, sir, Chief," Red said. Red opened the door to his trailer.

"Hey, Red!" Travis said. "You okay? You need a doctor? I can have Dr. Beth come out and take a look."

Red shook his head. "Naw, I'm okay. Just a little tired."

"Well, alright, then. You take it easy, Red."

Travis felt bad for the old man. Meth had taken everything away from him. His wife had taken the kids and left a long time ago because of the paranoia and hallucinations. She had awoken one night and he had a knife to her throat, asking who took his money. She left that night. He hadn't seen his kids in ten years. All he had was his mobile trailer, his social security check and his addiction.

Travis got the same story from the other three houses on the road. No, they hadn't seen any kids. No, they didn't know anything about a little girl. Yes, they were sure. No, they didn't need any help. Just wanted to be left alone.

The last place on his list was Earl Fields' house. The last time he'd been out this way, he'd been investigating a fire at Faye Collier's house. Earl had seemed nervous at the time, but that was because he dealt in meth and he knew that Travis knew. But Travis never had probable cause to search his place. Still, there was something about Earl that set Travis' warning senses on high.

Travis stepped up on the porch to knock on the door, which in itself was unusual. In the past, Earl had always met him before he reached the porch. He peeked though the screen door and saw Earl sitting at the table. Earl gave no sign he knew Travis was there. Odd. Earl had always been super aware of his surroundings. It's the hallmark of a criminal. Travis knocked once.

Earl jumped up and hurried to the door.

"Chief, I didn't hear you drive up! Come on in!" Earl said.

Now Travis knew something was going on. In the ten years he had been chief, Earl had never been friendly to him, much less invited him into his house.

"Want some coffee, Chief?" Earl asked. "I just made a fresh pot."

"Sure," Travis said. "I could use a cup."

"Sit down, sit down. I'll be just a minute," Earl said as he bustled to the coffee pot.

Travis sat on the torn, blue sofa. He remembered Tess' description of what had happened on a blue sofa. He could even see a couple of cigarette burns on the cushions. He tensed up. His eyes were hard as he looked up at Earl and took the coffee cup.

"So, Earl. You seen any little girls around the area?" he asked tersely.

Earl stammered. "Uh, uh, n-no, Chief. There ain't no kids round here. Why do you ask that?"

"Someone found a little girl over on the highway and she said she lived somewhere in the woods with a man that looks a lot like you," Travis said. He watched Earl closely.

"You don't say! Well, ain't that somethin'?" Earl declared. "It ain't me. I don't have nothin' to do with no kids. You know that, Travis. I like full grown women, ya know what I mean?"

"Yeah, I know what you mean, Earl. But I gotta check it out, ya know? You don't mind if I have a look around, do ya?"

Earl smiled confidently. "Hell, no, Chief! Look all you want. I ain't got nothin' to hide!"

It didn't take Travis long to search the small cabin. It was spotless. Someone had given it a good cleaning.

Even scrubbed the floors, it looked like. Travis saved the kitchen for last. This is where Tess had said the trap door to her room was.

Earl had sat on the sofa while Travis searched, not even watching him. When Travis moved to the kitchen, though, he stood up.

"Satisfied?" he asked.

"Just one more thing," Travis replied.

He moved the table to the side and lifted the rug to reveal the trap door. Earl looked nervous now. Travis flung open the door.

"Ain't nothin' down there but an empty root cellar, Chief," he said.

"Well, I still gotta take a look. You know. Cover all my bases, Earl."

Travis climbed down the rickety ladder into the small dark space. He imagined Tess living here all those years and his rage swelled inside of him. Someone had obviously cleaned up. The dirt floor actually had broom marks. There was no sign anyone had lived down here. Earl had done a good job covering up. He had found nothing that would tie him to Tess. He sighed and began to climb the ladder. As he gave the cellar a last glance, he noticed a small disturbed place in the back wall. He stepped back down off the ladder and inspected it closer. Someone had hidden something in the wall and covered it with dirt. He brushed the dirt away and pulled at the old rag that peeked out. It was a doll! A doll made out of rags. Just a simple toy, but one that would mean the world to a child with nothing. He slipped the doll under his vest and climbed up.

Earl had been pacing up in the kitchen. He stopped when Travis came up and slammed the trap door shut.

"You were right, Earl," he said. "Just an empty root cellar. Except for this." He held up the rag doll.

"Told you, Chief," Earl said. "I ain't got nothin' to hide. I don't know what that is or how it got there. Must be left over from the previous owners." Earl shuffled his feet nervously.

Travis stared at him and said, "That's odd you didn't find it before because it looks like that cellar has had a good cleaning recently, Earl."

Earl just shrugged his shoulders and stared at the floor.

Travis left Earl's place, knowing that Tess had been there. He knew Earl was the monster who had hurt her. But how could he prove it? Tess would have to identify him and she had been through enough. He didn't want to put her through that.

Travis hurried back to town. He wanted to show Tess the doll to confirm his suspicions. He had known

Earl was a mean son of a bitch. Earl had been in fights at the Booty Call several times, nearly killing his opponent each time. But he had always claimed self defense, so Travis couldn't arrest him. All the witness were too scared of Earl to contradict him. The poor drunks he had beaten couldn't remember anything, so Earl was free to go.

But this. Torturing this child! It was beyond Travis' comprehension that even Earl could do this. He made a silent promise to Tess that, if it was true, Earl would pay.

Tess was asleep when he got to the office. Beth asked if Travis would stay while she did a little shopping and checked on her office. After she left, Travis just stood in the doorway, watching the sleeping child.

He knew he needed to call the Child Services Department in Cleveland. He was trying to postpone it using the pretense that he needed to solve the crime first. He had seen children who went into the system at a young age. At five years old, Tess' age, they were malleable. Depending on the influences of the foster home, they could either go down the bad path or the good path. Very few went down the good path. Most of the children in the system were already adept at stealing and lying. The older ones were bullies to the younger ones, which in turn, forced the young ones to become the submissives in that toxic relationship. Travis didn't think Tess would survive another brutal situation.

The first thought of fostering Tess popped in his head. Beth and Travis had been engaged for two years. Neither felt any urgency to be married. They already knew they were meant for each other. The formalities could wait. They had talked about the future and both wanted children. Down the road. Several years down the road. Now, Travis was thinking, maybe sooner. First, he needed to find out if Tess had any family. Then, he would need to talk to Beth. Her practice was the newest one in town and it was slowly growing. She needed to focus on that before marriage. That's why the long engagement. Plus, a family of three could not live in the chief's apartment and Beth's place was a just a one-room studio. He had an old house he was renovating, but it wasn't quite ready yet. There were definitely obstacles.

He pushed that thought aside. First things first. Catching the son of a bitch was his priority.

While Tess was sleeping, Travis caught up on some paperwork and calls he had been neglecting. Coop had called to check on the child. Travis picked up the phone and dialed his number.

When Coop answered, he said, "Hey, Coop. This is Travis. I'm returnin' your call. Sorry it took so long."

"No worries, Travis. I just wanted to check on the little girl. How's she doin'?"

"She's doin' better," Travis replied. "I wanted to talk to you about that. Have you mentioned her to anyone?"

"Heck, no, Travis! I figured you'd want that kept under wraps until you could get a handle on things. Besides, you know I don't go anywhere other than the grocery," Coop replied.

"Well, I'd appreciate it if you kept it to yourself for a little while longer," Travis said. "At least until I catch the bastard that did this to her."

"Sure thing, Chief. Just let me know if you need help. I got my 12-gauge at the ready, just for him."

"Thanks, Coop. I'll let you know," Travis chuckled. In his mind, he imagined old Coop with his frail 80-year-old body and a shotgun up against 6'4" muscular Earl. But he did appreciate Coop's spirit.

He answered a few other calls. Dogs in the trash at Sue's diner. Broken down car on Hwy 61. A fight among the teens at the bowling alley. Little stuff. Par for crimes in Gnaw Bone.

As he finished up, Tess appeared in the doorway. Her hair was tousled and she was rubbing her eyes. She was holding on to the doll Beth had given her like it was her best friend.

"Where's Beth?" she asked.

"Beth had to go for a minute. She'll be back. You hungry?" Travis said as he crossed the room.

Tess nodded.

"Well, how about some eggs? I make the world's best eggs," he said.

"Better than Beth's?" she asked

"Well, maybe not better than her's. But pretty darn good," he laughed.

Tess smiled and nodded again. A warm feeling spread through him at her smile. Maybe he was making headway. He picked her up and carried her into the kitchen.

While they were eating, Travis asked Tess if she could remember anything about her mother.

"I think there was a woman when I was a baby," she said. "I cain't picture her, but I remember someone singin' to me."

Travis pulled out the dirty rag doll.

"I have somethin' to show you," he said. He held up the doll and watched her closely.

Tess stared at the doll. Her face was very solemn. She took the doll and looked at it carefully.

"It's mine," she whispered. "I had to hide her from the man so he wouldn't hurt her, too."

She looked up with tears in her eyes. "I think the woman gave her to me when I was very little."

That confirmed it. Earl had kept Tess in that dirty old root cellar. He had done horrible, unthinkable things to her. And he had probably killed Tess' mother. Travis felt rage. A rage he had never felt before. He was determined to bring him to justice.

But, for now, he picked up Tess and held her close. Tess was still holding the rag doll to her chest, dirt and all.

He put her down and said, "Come on, let's get you dressed. I want to take you for a ride."

Travis drove her out to County Road 1100 along the same path he had followed that morning. When he reached Red's mobile home, he slowed down.

"Tess, I want you to look at these houses and tell me if you've ever been here before."

She looked at Red's trailer and shook her head.

Each time, she looked at the shack and the area, shaking her head.

The only one left was Earl's house. As they were about to reach his driveway, Earl came barreling down the road in his big black truck. He slowed down when he noticed Travis's vehicle. Tess had heard the truck and immediately dropped down to the floorboard, a look of sheer terror on her face. She hunched over and covered her head.

Travis grabbed a coat from the back seat and covered her with it. Earl stopped alongside Travis.

"Chief," he said. "You headed to my place?"

"No," Travis said firmly. "I'm gonna park up here and walk through the woods a while. Thought I might go huntin' in a few days. You don't mind, do ya?"

"No, no. Go right ahead. Maybe you'll have better luck that I did yesterday," Earl replied, snickering at the hidden reference that only he understood.

Then he drove off, content that he had gotten Travis off his trail. That cleaning of his cabin had definitely payed off. He smiled as he headed to town.

Travis removed the coat and told Tess it was safe, to come on up. Tess was trembling. Even though she had fought Earl her entire life and never showed weakness, she was afraid. The last couple of days with Beth and Travis had been unlike anything she remembered. She was so afraid the man would find her and take her again.

She climbed back on the seat, looking all around for the truck. Travis asked her what was wrong.

"That was the man," she said. "I heard his truck and I got scared. Then when he stopped and talked, I knew his voice. I don't want him to take me!"

"Tess. I would never let him take you. You are safe with me. That man will never hurt you again. Please believe that," he whispered.

He put his arm around her and just sat there until she stopped trembling.

"Now, I have one other place to show you and then we can go home. Okay?"

Tess sniffled and nodded.

They pulled up to Earl's cabin. Tess slowly raised her head and looked at the place. There was no emotion on her face. She was very still.

Travis said, "Tess? Do you know this place?"

Ever so slightly, Tess nodded.

"This is where I lived with the man," she said.

That was all Travis needed. He backed up and returned to town. Satisfied that he had found the man who hurt Tess, he now needed help from the state police to prove it.

Chapter 16

Travis sent Tess off to watch TV and play with her dolls while he did a little work.

Travis got on the phone with the county DA. He laid out all the facts of Tess 'captivity and his suspicion that it was Earl. He was rewarded with a search and arrest warrant.

The next person he called was Captain George McNeely at the Mississippi State Police in Jackson. He and George had grown up together in Jackson and were best friends all through school. They joined the Army together when they graduated high school. Travis had specialized in criminal investigations while George became an MP canine handler. Although they were rarely stationed in the same place at the same time, they kept in touch over the years and reconnected when Travis joined the Jackson police force upon returning from the service.

George was now in charge of handling and training the state canine officers. He also worked closely with the human trafficking squad of the state police. He was married to his high school sweetheart, Alice, and they had three beautiful daughters.

George was glad to hear from Travis. "Travis, you old dog! How you been?"

"Oh, you know, George. Just livin the good life here in Gnaw Bone," Travis laughed. "How's Alice and the girls?"

Travis had dated Alice briefly before she met George. They had fun, but didn't really connect romantically. After she started dating George, they had remained good friends.

"They are fantastic," George replied. "Little Susie just got her first tooth! And Alice says you need to come visit. The girls miss their Uncle Travis."

"Someday soon, I promise. Right now, I need your help," Travis said.

Travis laid out what had happened over the past week and why he suspected Earl. He asked George if he could bring his dogs up to search Earl's place.

"I most definitely can," George declared. "We'll catch this bastard, Travis. I promise you. I'll be there tomorrow mornin'."

There had been no calls so far about trouble in town, so Travis thought about treating Tess to an outing. He knew he was chancing her being seen, but it was a beautiful day and kids were in school. The park would be empty. He wanted to bond more with Tess, so he decided to do it.

"Tess," he called. When she poked her head around the door, he said, "I have a treat for you. Wanna come with me?"

She nodded her head vigorously.

The park used to be in the center of town near the highway. It had been close to Jimmy's Drive In, a popular hangout for high school kids skipping school. The town had closed that park years ago because it also became a popular place for drug dealers. It had been rebuilt in a small, working class neighborhood, away from the main part of town. There were swings, monkey bars, see-saws and a splash pad. The park was dotted with huge sugar maples trees that provided shade to the entire area. The tennis courts were at one end and the basketball goals at the other. Travis had spent many an afternoon on those basketball courts.

Today, as he suspected, the park was empty. He asked Tess where she wanted to start. Tess looked at him blankly.

"What do you mean?" She had no idea what a park was.

Travis chuckled and said, "Come on. I'll show you."

He led her over to the merry-go-round and showed her how to sit and hold on to the bars. Then he started pushing her slowly at first and the faster as he saw her face light up. She giggled and yelled, "Faster! Faster!"

When she had her fill of whirling around on the merry-go-round, she wanted to try the swings. Travis pushed her progressively higher and higher with Tess laughing out loud the whole time. She enjoyed the monkey bars and splash pad just as much. She had never had so much fun.

They were sitting on the picnic table, resting, when Tess suddenly tensed up. She scooted close to Travis and tucked her head under his arm. Travis wondered what had happened to make her withdraw. Then he heard it too. Glass packs. He looked up and saw Earl's black truck coming off a side street onto the drive that circled the park.

It was too late to hide Tess. Earl drove slowly by, staring at her. When Travis picked her up and put her in the truck, he faced Earl's direction, his hand on his weapon. Earl sped away, blowing black smoke from the glass packs. Travis thought tomorrow couldn't come soon enough. He didn't think Earl would try anything while he was around, but he couldn't be sure. He wanted this to end.

Tess was silent on the ride home. She hurried into the bedroom and crawled under the covers. Beth was there and had started supper. Fried chicken, green beans and mashed potatoes. Travis' favorite. She saw Tess run into the bedroom and close the door. Travis came in right after.

"What on earth happened?" she asked him.

Travis told her all he had discovered today and that Earl was definitely the one who had hurt Tess. She sat down, stunned. She and Earl had gone to the same high school in Cleveland, but she didn't know him well. She had been a couple of years behind him. She knew he had dropped out in his junior year. And he had a reputation of bullying kids smaller than him. But that was it. He had never been to her clinic and she hadn't interacted with him at all.

"What are you going to do," she asked.

"I'm going to search his place tomorrow," he replied. "Right now, I need more evidence. Tess' story isn't enough."

He told her about George and their plans for tomorrow. Beth was relieved that Travis wasn't going after him alone. She trusted George and knew that he would have Travis' back.

Travis and George started out at daylight. George had brought along his top search dog, Arman. Arman was a Belgian Malinois trained for search/rescue and pursuit/takedown. He was a gentle dog, especially around children. He only became vicious when given the Czech command "Zadrrz" (pronounced zad-rish) by George. Then, he became a 100-lb missile zeroed in on his target. He would barrel toward his target and latch onto his arm or leg to bring him down. He would continue the vicious attack until George uttered the release command "Pust" (pronounce poost). Most of the time, the target sustained serious injuries. Arman jumped up in the back of the chief's truck and curled up in a ball. He knew he would be working soon.

The men were quiet on the ride to Earl's shack, lost in their own thoughts. Travis was furious at the things that had been done to Tess. He was determined to get justice for her. George was not immune to the feelings that Travis was feeling, but he had learned to control them. He was concentrating on the task at hand, catching the perp. Both were hoping Arman would be find some evidence that Tess had been held at Earl's place.

They pulled up in front of the shack. The big, black truck was in the driveway, but there was no sign of Earl.

Travis walked up on the crickety old porch and knocked on the door. No answer. He peeked through the windows. Earl was nowhere in sight. George held the shirt Tess had been found in under Arman's nose.

"Revier."

As soon as he whispered in the search command in the dog's ear, Arman began working. Sniffing every nook and cranny of the yard. He hit on a couple of spots, but quickly moved on. Tess had not been allowed in the yard so her scent wasn't strong there.

Travis knocked on the door again. "Earl," he yelled. "I have a search warrant." Still no answer. Travis tried the doorknob. It rattled, but did not open. Travis backed up and kicked it open.

The instant Arman passed through the doorway, he sat down. Tess' scent was everywhere. Still, George led him around the house, sniffing and whining. He hit on the couch, bed, kitchen table and trapdoor. Arman had confirmed Travis' suspicion that Earl was the one who had hurt Tess, but there was still no physical proof.

Only Tess could identify him. And he wasn't ready to put her through that yet.

Chapter 17

Earl was back in the hollers at his meth lab when Travis and George searched his house.

He had packed up his product and began the hike back home. He was just topping the ravine when he noticed Travis' vehicle in front of his house. He crouched down and watched. They must be in the house, he thought. Just then, he saw Travis step out onto the porch. Right behind him was a large man with a large dog. He lay flat on the ground and peeked through the brush, hoping they didn't see him.

Just as George and Arman stepped out, Arman's ears stood straight up. He looked toward the ravine behind the house and whined. Both George and Travis turned to see what had his attention. Suddenly, Arman growled. It was low and menacing. His body was tense and all his attention was focused on the ravine.

Earl lay flat on the ground and started quietly scooting back down the ravine. The dog had sensed him.

George knew Arman well enough to know that he wouldn't alert on something that wasn't something. He scoured the edge of the ravine with his eyes and didn't see anything. But he trusted Arman. He unleashed him and whispered, "Zadrrz!"

Arman took off like a bullet, straight for the ravine. He barreled over the edge with George and Travis right behind him. Earl had managed to get halfway down the ravine. When he saw Arman racing toward him, he stood and ran. That was the wrong thing to do. Arman loved to chase his prey. Earl had only run twenty feet before Arman jumped and latched onto his arm. Earl screamed and started shaking his arm trying to get Arman to release. But Belgian Malinois dogs have a bite force of about 224 pounds, close to a pit bull's bite, and are not easy to repel. Earl fell to the ground and tried to cover his head with his other arm. He curled up in the fetal position. Arman straddled him, still holding on to his arm. Travis and George scrambled down to them. As Travis grabbed Earl, George said, "Pust."

Arman immediately released Earl's arm and sat by George, still watching his prey.

The bag of meth was draped over Earl's shoulder. Travis saw the product inside and jerked Earl around. He was not gentle in handcuffing him. He may not be able to prove what he did to Tess, but he at least had him on drugs with intent to distribute. That should put him away for a good long while.

"Well, Earl, this is not your lucky day," Travis said.

He looked at George.

"I have to take him to the county jail in Cleveland. I'll take you back to your truck first, though."

George nodded. He patted Arman on the head and gave him a biscuit. He had done his job.

At the office, Travis did not take Earl out of the truck while he said goodbye to George. He didn't want to chance Tess seeing him. As soon as George was gone, he drove Earl over to the town clinic and had his bite injuries patched up. Beth, of course, was taking care of Tess, but the nurse did a good job of disinfecting and wrapping Earl's arm.

The ride to Bolivar County Jail in Cleveland took about an hour. Travis glanced at Earl in the rear view mirror. Earl was resting, his head leaning back on the car seat, eyes closed. Travis thought, it's incomprehensible God would create someone so evil as to harm a child as he had harmed Tess.

"Earl, how did you end up with Tess?" he asked.

"I don't know what you're talkin' about, Chief," Earl replied. "Who's Tess?"

It was true. Earl had never known her name. Nor had he cared.

Travis stared at him hard. Earl was an accomplished liar and rarely let his emotions show. He was a hard read.

"It's the little girl I found on the road who says she lived with you," he said.

"Oh, her!" Earl laughed. "I didn't kidnap her, if that's what you think. She was payment for some product I sold to old Faye. Faye Collier. It was a couple years ago, I guess."

"What kind of product?"

"Now, Travis. I ain't gonna tell you that," Earl smirked.

Travis could guess since he had a bag of it next to him on the seat.

"So, where did Faye get her?" he asked.

"Her kid, Jody, had her. Faye didn't want a baby around, so you can guess the rest." Earl was relaxed as if on a Sunday joy ride. He'd been in jail before. He knew what to expect.

"Where's Jody?" Travis asked.

At that question, Earl sat up, eyes locked with Travis.

"Uh, I don't know nothin' about Jody," he said. "She wasn't with Faye when we did the deal." He looked down.

The rest of the ride was silent. Travis was lost in his thoughts. So, Tess was Jody's daughter. He'd always liked Jody. The poor girl never had much of a chance with Faye as a mom. But she was no druggie and had done well in school until she dropped out. She'd never been in any trouble that Travis knew of. He knew she was a prostitute, but in his mind, that was a victimless crime. It's the only way some people could make a living, so he rarely ever picked them up. As far as he knew, Faye was the only kin that Jody had. He would have to find Jody. For Tess.

Travis booked Earl into the county jail on drug possession with intent. He would need to come back the next day for the arraignment and then later for the trial. But for now, Tess was safe from Earl and that was enough.

Chapter 18

Tess smiled and waved when Travis walked in. She had now been with him almost a week and was warming up to him. Of course, she loved Beth. But trusting Travis, another man, had been hard. Slowly, she was letting down her guard with him, though.

She was having a tea party with her dolls. She was sipping Kool-Aid and eating crackers. Beth had told her earlier about the tea parties she had had as a child. Tess asked Beth to show her how. She'd been busy all afternoon after that. Beth was cooking dinner. She looked anxiously at Travis and mouthed, "How'd it go?"

He nodded his head as he hugged her waist and kissed her cheek. "Good," he whispered.

Tess brought her dolls to the table with her and pretended to feed them as she ate. She had never had dolls before. She felt like they were her best friends, which she had never had either. Travis and Beth were quietly talking amongst themselves, every once in a while asking Tess a question or just smiling at her. She liked it here. She hoped she could always stay here.

As Beth cleared the dishes, Travis took Tess' hand. He looked solemnly into her eyes. Tess was nervous. He was going to tell her bad news, she thought.

"Tess, the man who hurt you is named Earl. Earl Fields. I went out to his house today and arrested him. He's gonna to be in jail for a long time. I think you are safe now," Travis said.

Tess looked down. She thought for a minute. She hadn't been worried about the man, Earl, taking her as long as Travis and Beth were around. She felt so safe with them. It took her a minute to absorb the fact that Earl was no longer a threat. That she could go anywhere with anyone and still be safe. Suddenly, she leapt up and threw her arms around Travis' neck.

"Thank you, Travis," she said quietly.

Travis felt the tears well in his eyes as he hugged the tiny body. This little girl had just grabbed his heart and held on.

"You are certainly welcome, Tess," he whispered.

That night, after Tess had gone to bed, Travis and Beth went out to his office so Tess couldn't hear them.

Travis sighed. "Now that Earl is gone and Tess is safe, I have to turn her over to Child Services in Cleveland."

The tears ran silently down Beth's face.

"Travis, you can't. I can't bear to let her go!" she said. "Isn't there some other way?"

Travis reached over and held her hand.

"I don't see one," he said. "She has a mother. Earl told me that Jody Collier is her mom. Until I find her, Tess needs a stable home. She needs to be in school. She needs a normal life. Child Services can give that to her."

"But, can't we give that to her?"

Travis stared at her. It had crossed his mind, but he wasn't sure how Beth would feel. Until now, they had both been content with just being engaged. A future promise. No hurry. But, it had been two years of engagement. Was she ready to take the final step?

"Why, Ms. Rhodes, are you sayin' what I think you are sayin'," he asked, a quizzical smile on his lips.

"Well, I don't know," Beth stammered. "Am I? It would be a solution, don't you think?"

"It might be. I'd have to check with Child Services to see if we can even have her. Are you sure?" he said.

"Travis, I love you. You love me. We've been engaged for two years. We both love Tess. We are just movin' up the timetable, that's all. Please. Marry me," she begged.

He kissed her longingly on the lips. "Okay," he whispered. "I'll check with Child Services first thing in the mornin'."

Travis decided to visit Child Services in person. He was sitting outside their offices in Cleveland at 7 a.m. the next morning. The building was a typical public service building. Brick on the outside, painted institutional green on the inside. The well worn floors were linoleum, gray and white checkered tile, covered with years of scuff stains. It was a sad place. No place for children.

The matronly woman stomping toward him looked angry. Her half blonde, half gray hair was pulled up in a bun at top of her head. She was wearing a dull gray skirt with matching jacket and an off white blouse. She ignored him as she unlocked the office door, entered, shut the door and relocked it. Travis was astonished. Had she not seen him sitting there? Of course, she had! It was 7:30 and the office opened at eight. Was she really going to let him sit there until exactly eight o'clock? He was tempted to bang on the door, but he didn't want to start off on the wrong foot. Beth would never forgive him if he blew this.

The minutes seemed to drag by. He could hear the clock on the wall, tick, tick, tick. At exactly eight o'clock, he heard the door lock click. He rose and collected himself before he went in. Inside the office was no more cheerful than outside. Same dull green walls. The office furniture was a dirty cream color. The woman who had entered earlier was sitting at a cluttered desk, covered in file folders and papers. Her nameplate read "Ms. Mildred Walker". She ignored him.

He stood at the counter a minute or so before she looked up.

"May I help you?" she asked. There was no "customer service" tone to her voice. It was flat, irritated. Like he had invaded her private space.

Travis cleared his throat. "Yes, ma'am," he said. "I'd like to see about fosterin' a child."

She stared at him and took a long drink of her coffee.

"I don't do fosterin'," she said and went back to the papers on her desk.

Travis stood there a moment. "Well, is there someone else who can help me?"

"You'll have to wait until the director gets here at nine," she said.

Well, this is going just peachy, Travis thought. He settled in a chair near the door and waited. At exactly nine o'clock, a young man practically burst through the door. Travis recognized him as a kid who had graduated from Gnaw Bone High School about six years ago. He was dressed in a snazzy suit and wearing black and white wing tip shoes.

"Good mornin', Mildred!" he gushed in a cheerful voice. "Isn't today beautiful?"

Mildred just grunted and pointed to Travis.

"Chief Travis Hampton," Travis said as he extended his hand to the man.

"Chief!" the man said. He grabbed Travis' hand and pumped it several times. "I remember you!"

"Yeah, I thought I recognized you, too," Travis said. "Didn't you live in Gnaw Bone?"

"Yes, I did," he said. "Marvin Shaw. Call me Marvin. Come on into my office. Want some coffee?"

"That would be great," Travis answered, relieved that Marvin was in a much better mood than Mildred.

"Mildred!" Marvin shouted. "Get the man a coffee!"

Mildred stared hard at Travis and didn't move. Travis swallowed and looked away. Travis was afraid of nothing but this woman scared him a little. She sighed loudly as she rose from her chair and poured him a cup of coffee. She slowly walked into the office and sighed again as she handed it to Travis. She wanted him to know what an imposition it was.

"Thank you, Mildred," Travis mumbled.

Mildred grunted and shuffled back to her desk. She did not smile.

"You'll have to excuse Mildred, Chief," Marvin chuckled. "She's been here a million years and seen it all. Now, how can I help you?"

Travis proceeded to tell Marvin the circumstances of Tess' life and how she come to be with Travis. Marvin was shocked. He dealt with all kinds of child abuse in his line of work, but this was the worst case he had heard of. He wasn't sure how to handle it.

"Damn, Chief," he said. "Just damn. How is the little girl?"

"She's doin' okay," Travis answered. "She's settled in real good with my fiancé and me. I know you have to place her, but I'd really like to keep her with me. At least until I locate her mother."

Marvin hesitated. There was a lengthy procedure to become a foster parent. Most people did it for the extra income the state paid them per child. Marvin didn't like placing too many children in the same home, but with the shortage of foster parents, he had no choice.

"Chief. You know there's a procedure for these things. I can't just let you keep the child. You are single. And in a dangerous line of work. Who's gonna to take care of her while you are workin'?" Marvin asked.

"That's just it," Travis said. "Beth and I are gettin' married this weekend. She's a doctor. Tess has bonded with both of us. To rip her away from the only safe, stable place she's ever known would be cruel. It's only logical that she remain with us temporarily."

Marvin considered Travis' proposal. He did have a shortage of homes. And the little girl had already been through hell. Could he morally put her through another one when she had a good home already? He didn't think so. But, still, there are rules.

"I tell you what, Chief," he said. "I have to do a background check on both you and your lady friend. If y'all pass those, I'll let you keep her until you find her mother. But once you find her, it'll be a different story. The courts always lean toward the biological parents, if possible."

Travis breathed a big sigh. "I know, Marvin. I really appreciate this. Are there papers I need to sign or somethin'?"

"Not yet. We'll do all that when the background checks come back. By then, you'll be married and everything will be kosher. I'll need to come out and check the home environment first. How does next Tuesday work for you?"

They rose and shook hands.

"That will be just fine, Marvin. Thank you so much!" Travis beamed.

He gave Marvin the address and left. He couldn't wait to tell Beth and Tess.

Chapter 19

In his spare time, before Tess, Travis had been remodeling an old Colonial Revival home that he purchased at a real estate auction when he first moved to Gnaw Bone. His thought had been that he and Beth would live there when they got married. He had the downstairs about finished. He just needed to finish replacing the trim and furnish the place. The upstairs had not been touched. But the downstairs could be livable in no time.

The house was large. It was red brick with an elaborate entry door. Windows were evenly spaced on each side of the door. There was a portico over the doorway held up by two large round columns. Downstairs consisted of three bedrooms, two baths, a huge kitchen, a living room, an office and a laundry room. Upstairs had three more bedrooms and another bathroom. Travis had replaced all the floors with old hardwood. The walls had been painted using period colors and he had worked painstakingly to clean up the original trim and hardware. He had modernized the kitchen and opened the wall between the kitchen and dining room for a more open feel.

The only thing left to do was the furnishings. They had five days before Marvin would show up to inspect. Travis had no furnishings of his own. Everything in his apartment stayed with the apartment. Beth had a few things, but not enough to fill the place. They had decided on a shopping trip the next day. It would be fun to let Tess pick out her own furnishings. Both Beth and Tess had been ecstatic over his news about the foster care and about moving to the new place. They showed up at the house just as Travis was finishing for the day.

Beth had helped Travis many times with the remodeling, but this was the first time Tess had seen her new home. She had so many questions, the first being, "Where's my room?"

Travis scooped her up and gave her a grand tour. When they reached her room, he put her down and she explored every corner, even the closet. She looked back at Travis with tears in her eyes.

"No dirt?" she asked.

"No, honey," he said softly. "No dirt. And no trapdoor."

Tess looked around the room once more. "It'll do," she said and smiled.

Both Travis and Beth burst out laughing. It was good to see Tess showing a little sass. She had been sad for too long.

The Cleveland Furniture Store was a 2000 square foot furniture megaplex. There were two floors of any type of furniture one might need. It didn't take long to pick out the few pieces that they needed to furnish their room and the rest of the common areas. The excitement came when it was time to pick out Tess' furniture. She had to try every child's bed on the floor. Several times. She picked the princess canopy bed, of course, with pink bedding and ruffles on the canopy top. She chose a white oak, five drawer matching dresser with little glass knobs. Lastly, she chose a pink and white vanity desk with an oval mirror lined with pink wooden bows. Before leaving, Travis made arrangements to have the furniture delivered on Friday.

After the furniture spree, they had lunch at the 50's style diner in the town square. It felt good to be able to go out as a family for a change. There was no longer a threat to Tess, so this was their new normal.

Travis sat in the town square park while Beth and Tess visited the dress shop a few doors down. Since it was wedding related, he had been forbidden to accompany them. He liked people watching better than shopping anyway. He would pick a stranger and make up a story about them in his head. Of course, he didn't know if he was even close with his story, but it was fun to guess what that person was like. About an hour later, the girls returned, bags in hand, ready to go. He knew better than to ask to see what was in the bags. It had been a long day and Tess fell asleep before they hit the city limits.

The furniture was delivered on Friday and they spent the rest of the day making the house a home. Multiple shopping trips to Wal-Mart brought curtains, bedding, dishes, rugs, towels, etc. Tess was a little general, ordering Travis and Beth around, telling them where to put her furniture, and criticizing them if they did it wrong. Travis erected a barrier at the stairway to make the upstairs inaccessible until he could finish it. He didn't want Tess to explore the unfinished area and end up getting hurt. By Saturday morning, the house was ready.

Saturday afternoon, Beth and Travis were married at the Christian Congregational Church. Tess and the pastor's wife were the only ones in attendance. Travis wore his best suit. He looked so handsome, with his dark hair and glittering blue eyes. He stood at the front of the church with the pastor, shuffling from one foot to the other. He was nervous.

Tess came through the doors at the back with a bounce. She was wearing a flouncy white dress covered in ribbons and bows. Her blond hair had been pulled back and tied with a white satin ribbon. She carried a small white pillow topped with red rose petals and the wedding bands. She was all smiles as she skipped up the aisle and stood by Travis.

Beth wore a white lace floor length dress that clung to her curves. The V-neck bodice was covered in sparkling glitter, as was her veil. She actually shimmered walking down the aisle. Travis could barely speak. Of course, he knew Beth was beautiful, but nothing had prepared him for this beyond gorgeous bride coming toward him. The pastor leaned over and whispered, "Close your mouth, Travis." He did. But he couldn't take his eyes off Beth.

The ceremony was simple. The pastor's wife played the wedding march on the church organ. They exchanged vows and rings, kissed and it was done. To their surprise, the church bells began ringing as they were leaving and there was a small crowd of townspeople waiting outside the church. Travis guessed that the pastor or, more likely, his wife, had leaked the wedding news. The crowd cheered and threw rice as the couple and Tess walked to Beth's car. Sue was waiting for them at the car. She hugged Travis and then Beth. After Earl had been arrested, word had spread throughout town about Tess. Sue knelt down and hugged Tess.

"Welcome to Gnaw Bone, Tess," she whispered in her ear. "My name is Sue and if you ever need anythin', you can find me right over there." She pointed toward her diner.

Tess was uncomfortable with the stranger and moved closer to Travis. Sue chuckled.

"That's OK," she said. "You'll get to know me soon enough."

Travis helped Beth in the car so her dress didn't get damaged and turned to Sue.

"Thank you for that, Sue," he said.

Sue nodded and took hold of his arm. "Travis, I can take care of Tess tonight if you and Beth want to be alone."

"That's real nice of you, Sue. But I think Tess is still too skittish right now. It'll be fine. I appreciate the offer, though," he said.

The whole crowd waved as they drove toward their new home. When they got home, another surprise awaited. While they were at the church, Sue and others had laid out a feast on the table. There was roast beef, mashed potatoes and green beans. There was a strawberry pie for dessert. Wine was open and chilling and candles were lit. It was picture perfect.

By eight o'clock, Tess was exhausted and ready for her new bed. Travis carried her in and laid her in the bed. By the time he and Beth said their good nights and kissed her on the head, she was sound asleep. It had been a big day.

Travis lit a fire in the fireplace while Beth poured them some wine. They settled on the couch, watching the fire, thinking of all that had happened over the last couple of weeks. Travis took the wine glasses and set them aside. He slowly ran his fingers down Beth's face. He leaned over and kissed her softly on the lips. He could feel the fire in her. He kissed her neck while unzipping her dress. He took her hand and led her to the rug in front of the fireplace. He finished undressing her, all the while kissing her body. Beth removed his shirt, running her hands over his taut, lean chest and muscled arms. His breath quickened when she pushed his trousers down and began rubbing him. When they were undressed, Travis gently lay her on the rug. She reached for him. He entered her hard. They were both ready. They climaxed together. Travis held her tenderly in his arms as they fell asleep in front of the fire. Later in the night, he picked her up and carried her to bed. At last, they were home.

Marvin showed up, as promised, early Tuesday morning. Both Travis and Beth had passed the background checks with flying colors, of course. Marvin had rushed the foster parent paperwork through and was pleased to tell them they had been approved. He marveled at the house and the work Travis had done.

"I remember this old place," he said. "We used to come here as high school kids when it was abandoned and have parties!"

He looked at Travis, sheepishly. Those had been some wild parties. He suspected Travis may have found remnants of the beer bottles and was suddenly ashamed. Travis showed no reaction.

"Yes, I can imagine," he chuckled. "We did that in Jackson, too. But I've done a lot of work and you can see that it is a perfect home for us."

"Oh, yeah, no worries about that," Marvin said. "As long as you keep the stairway sealed off until the upstairs is done, you'll be fine."

Marvin had them sign the foster papers as he prepared to leave. He asked Travis, "Any luck with findin' the mom?"

Travis shook his head. "Not yet. I'll do all I can, but she's been missin' for two years."

He looked around for Tess. She was in her room and out of earshot. "I suspect she's been killed, but I have no proof."

Marvin nodded. "Do a good faith search for her. If you haven't found her in seven years, you can apply to adopt Tess if you want to. But do all you can to find her, Travis."

"I will, Marvin."

They shook hands and Marvin left.

Travis lingered outside on the porch thinking about the changes over the last month. Although it had happened suddenly, he was pleased that he and Beth were finally married and living in a home of their own. He was also happy Tess had burst into his life, even under such horrible circumstances. He hope that Earl would suffer as much as Tess had.

Chapter 20

Once Earl had been convicted and sentenced to 20 years in Parchman Prison, life began to return to normal for Travis and Beth. They both went back to work while Tess went to kindergarten. Tess blossomed. As it turned out, she was quite intelligent. She caught onto reading quickly. She always had her nose in a book. It was as if she couldn't learn fast enough. She was also feisty. Some of the kids had tried bullying her the first week or so, calling her an orphan, pushing her around. But she was having none of it. If they pushed her, she pushed back harder. Their taunts didn't rile her in the least. She just smiled and said, "Thank you." Not getting the fear response they were seeking, the other kids eventually left her alone.

She was not part of the popular clique. She didn't like the way they treated the kids who were less fortunate. They treated them either like they didn't exist or like they were bugs, meant to be squashed under the expensive Jordans they wore. No one knew Tess' past. Just that she had no parents and lived with the police chief and his wife. The fact that she was an orphan placed her squarely in the underclass as far as the clique was concerned. That was okay with Tess. She preferred hanging out with the outcasts.

One day there there was a Brazilian Jiu-Jitsu demonstration at school. Tess recognized some of the kids in the demonstration as the nerdy ones in her class. They were like her, only meeker and milder. They loved to learn. And because of that, they were often bullied by the clique.

Tess loved everything about the demonstration. The white Gi (pronounced "ghee" with a hard "g") uniform, the different colored belts, the sharp, quick movements. Mostly, she loved the strength and power of jiu-jitsu. Even the smallest person could be mighty and defend themselves. It appealed to her because, although she felt entirely safe with Travis and Beth, she still felt vulnerable.

Beth usually picked Tess up from school and took her back to the clinic with her. On this day, Tess ran and jumped in the back seat more excited than Beth had ever seen her.

"There was this jitsu thing at school today! It was so cool! The kids were little like me and they were fightin' and beatin' the big kids! They had these cool uniforms and belts and were barefoot! I want lessons, Beth! Please, please, please!" Tess gushed.

Beth was taken aback by her exuberance.

"Well, uh, Tess, we'll talk to Travis about it tonight," she stammered.

Of course, Travis thought it was a good idea. He knew Tess needed to feel in control and safe. Jiu-jitsu might be just the answer.

She began classes the next week. Her instructor was a woman named Keri Stone. Keri came from Cleveland once a week to hold classes at the community center. She was an average woman, 30 yrs old, about 5'4" tall, weight around 120 lbs. She had thick brown hair and chocolate brown eyes. She appeared to be part Choctaw, the Native American tribe that still resides on a large reservation near Jackson. The class had about 15 kids in it, along with Tess. Most of them knew Tess and gladly welcomed her.

If Tess wasn't doing her homework or reading, she was practicing her jiu-jitsu moves. She became quite proficient and moved up the belts rapidly. She had made friends with the other kids in the class, but it was clear she was the alpha personality. She wasn't mean and she didn't bully, but the others looked up to her. She was a natural leader.

Chapter 21

Parchman Farm, also known as the Mississippi State Penitentiary, is the oldest prison in the state and also the state's only maximum security prison for men. It houses nearly 3,500 inmates and the state execution chamber. It is known as one of the toughest prisons in the country.

Parchman is situated in the Mississippi Delta on 18,000 acres of prime farm ground. Inmates work ten hour days, six days a week working in fields of cotton, soybeans, and other cash crops. They also raise cattle, swine and chickens. Inmates live in long, single story dormitories, built from brick and lumber produced on-site. Each dormitory holds one hundred twin size cots. Each inmate's 8'x10' space contains the bed, a footlocker and a side table with a lamp. There is no barrier between the beds. It is just a large open room. The floors are wooden planks, worn smooth after decades of use. The walls are a drab gray color. Some blue spots showed through, left over from the last fresh paint job over 30 years ago. Windows line the wall facing the yard. They open to allow ventilation in the dorm. There is no air conditioning and very little heat in the winter.

Visiting day is different from the other days when there are no visitors. On visiting day, the room is filled with families and inmates. Children's laughter mixes with the murmuring voices of the adults. It is in stark contrast to the yelling and cursing between inmates on a regular day. On regular days, there are always fights, sometimes with injuries. And hip hop or rap music plays loudly all night until lights out at 10:00 p.m. The men play cards for chits. The chit could represent a carton of cigarettes, a pair of shoes or canteen credit. Just like the outside world, there are consequences if one reneges on a chit, the deadliest being a shiv to an organ.

Earl thought he would like Parchman. He didn't mind hard work and he thrived on violence. He had been processed in and assigned a cot in the middle of the row. The inmates were all out in the fields until supper time. When they came shuffling in around five o'clock, they were dusty and tired. They barely noticed Earl. The population in his dorm was probably about seventy percent black and thirty percent white. Earl didn't know their crimes. It was considered rude to ask and being rude could get him killed.

There was always an alpha dog in groups like this, and, in this case, that dog was Tyrone. He was a huge black man who stood 6'6" tall and weighed three hundred pounds. There was no fat on Tyrone. He was all muscle from working the fields and weight lifting in the yard. Earl knew he was the alpha as soon as Tyrone walked into the dorm. The other inmates parted to let him through and they all looked at the floor as he passed. There was no mistaking the power this man held over them. Tyrone stopped at Earl's cot and looked him over good. Earl stared back, too dumb to look away. Tyrone gave him a hint of a smile and walked on. Earl released the breath he didn't realize he had been holding.

He was asleep when someone grabbed him and clamped a hand over his mouth. He struggled but there were three of them and he couldn't move. They dragged him into the shower room at the end of the dorm. Three large black men took turns thrusting themselves into Earl until he passed out. They left him lying in his own blood on the hard bathroom floor. When he came to later that night, he crawled to his cot. Tyrone pursed his lips and made a kissing sound as he crawled by.

Being the new fish in the house, Earl was on the bottom of the inmate hierarchy. The other inmates stole his food, blankets, shoes. He was beaten every day. They would catch him in the cattle barn, beat him up and leave him face down in the manure pile. They began calling him "Stinky" because the odor would not leave him. The guards turned a blind eye to what was happening to him. As far as they were concerned, the sooner he fell in line, the easier his time would be. More than likely, they were paid to look the other way.

This brutality was a new experience for Earl. He was usually the one delivering the brutality, not receiving it. He had always been the alpha personality. He bullied; he did not get bullied. He raped; he didn't get raped. And he didn't like it. Somehow, he had to regain his power. And soon.

Earl decided to make his move during yard time. This was an hour a day when inmates could relax in the prison yard. Some played cards, some sat alone and enjoyed solitude. Others worked out with the weights. Others played basketball. Tyrone always lifted weights.

Earl was playing basketball when the Tyrone and two of his lackeys began lifting weights next to the court. It was a rough game. Lots of elbows being thrown; players being tripped. The cheering on the sideline from the other inmates encouraged even rougher play. Earl had the ball and was charging toward the goal. Instead of shooting, he intentionally slammed the ball into Tyrone's head.

Instantly, the yard fell silent. Everyone's eyes were on Tyrone as he rose slowly from the weight bench, his black body gleaming with sweat. His muscles were flexing and he was furious. Earl squared up to him. He was a couple inches shorter and about a hundred pounds lighter, but he was faster and quicker on his feet. His years as a torturer had taught him the weakness of a human body.

Earl attacked first, jabbing a fist in Tyrone's throat. Although Tyrone coughed, it didn't stop him from throwing a big haymaker swing toward Earl. Earl jumped back and kicked Tyrone in the testicles. As he bent over, holding his package, Earl swung an uppercut into his chin. That flattened Tyrone on his back. Earl straddled him and gouged at his eyes with his thumbs. Tyrone held up his hands as if to say, "No more." Earl took his homemade shiv and jammed it deep into Tyrone's neck. When he pulled it out, arterial blood began spurting from the wound. Tyrone was dead in a matter of seconds. Earl stood up and faced the crowd that had gathered to cheer them on. Then he turned to face Tyrone's two lackeys. They raised their palms and backed away. Earl knew he would have no more trouble from anyone. He had proved his dominance. He melted into the crowd, which dispersed as the guards came running.

Life at Parchman was easy for Earl after the fight. He was given extra food in the chow line. Inmates gave him cigarettes and homemade moonshine in exchange for protection. They always let him win at cards. But the best thing, in Earl's mind, was he had plenty of captive prey for his games. He had never tortured men before. Turned out, he enjoyed men just as much as women. But he never forgot the little bitch that had caused him to be here. He dreamt of paying her back one day. And that meant a little extra cruelty to the poor souls who were his victims now.

He had moved to the cot farthest from the door which separated the inmates from the night guard, next to the showers. Here he had a bit more privacy. There were plenty of inmates in his dorm who provided sex willingly to the others. They wore their shirts tied around their midriffs and their pants low around their hips for quick access. They would slink around the dorm, selling their bodies in exchange for cigarettes and moonshine. Earl wanted nothing to do with them. No, he wanted the most masculine inmates in the dorm. He would walk over to his chosen victim for the night and touch him on the shoulder. Willing or not, the inmate would accompany him to Earl's cot. Fearing they would be next, the others kept their eyes averted. They didn't want to know what was happening.

Earl would start out by stripping the inmate and tying him spread eagle and face down to the bed. He would shove a rag into their mouth to quell the screaming. In the beginning, he would touch the lit cigarettes indiscriminately all over the body, especially the private parts. The smell of burning flesh was an aphrodisiac to him. As time went on, he took to burning his initials into their skin. He liked the idea that he was branding them, making them his property. When he finished with the torture, he would rape them, roughly. Then he would push them off his bed and fall asleep. The brutalized inmate would shuffle, sometimes crawl, back to his own bunk and sob.

Yes, prison life was good for Earl.

Chapter 22

Travis spent part of every day trying to locate Jody. Over time, he called every police station and sheriff's office in the state inquiring about her. Have you any information on a petite, 18-yr-old female, blonde hair, blue eyes? Are there any unidentified female bodies in your morgue? Do you have anyone named Jody Collier in your district? He would always follow up the phone calls by faxing a missing poster of Jody for them to distribute. If there was an unidentified white female body, he would take the day and travel to the morgue to see if it was Jody. It never was.

Tess had asked about her parents right after the kids at school started taunting her for being a orphan.

"Travis," she said. "What is an orphan?"

"Well, honey, it's when someone doesn't have a mommy or daddy."

"But I'm not an orphan! You and Beth are my mommy and daddy!" she declared.

"No, Tess," said Travis. "We are not. We are your foster parents because we wanted to take care of you. We love you, but we are not your real parents."

Tess thought about this for a moment. "Then where are my real parents?"

"Your mama's name is Jody Collier. I've been lookin' for her but haven't found her yet. I don't know who your real daddy is, sweetie."

"So, if you find Jody, will I have to go live with her?" Tess' lip was quivering now.

"Aw, don't be thinkin' about that right now. I have to find her first and then we'll figure it out." Travis picked her up and hugged her tight. "Okay?"

"Okay," she said and hugged him back.

It had been three years since Travis had rescued her from Earl. She rarely thought about him anymore. Occasionally, he would surface in her dreams as a large, shadowy figure chasing her through the woods. His evil face would materialize out of the shadow and laugh. Every time he reached out to grab her, she would awaken with a jolt and look around her room frantically. As soon as she realized where she was, she would calm down. Sometimes, she would tiptoe to Travis and Beth's room and sneak in to sleep on the floor at the foot of their bed. She didn't tell them about the dreams.

She came to the breakfast table one morning, still mulling over one of those dreams. She sat down across the table from Beth and Travis, who were acting unusually squirrelly. She looked at them quizzically. They were glancing at each other and trying not to smile. Then they would glance at Tess. Then back at each other and giggle.

"All right," she said as she slammed her hand on the table. "That's enough! What in tarnation is goin' on?"

They burst out laughing.

"You caught us, Tess," Beth laughed. "We were goin' to tell you tonight."

"Tell me what?"

Travis took her hand. "You are gonna to have a brother or sister this spring."

Tess was stunned. She sat there, mouth open, staring at the two of them. A baby? The thought had never entered her mind. She started smiling. A real live baby! She jumped up and ran to hug them.

"When?! I can't wait," she said. "Boy or girl? What's the name gonna to be? Can I name it? I hope it's a girl. No, I hope it's a boy! No, a girl! Oh, I don't care! We have to get the baby room ready!"

Tess was giddy with delight all day. During library period, she checked out books all about babies. She couldn't wait to show them to Beth. That evening at dinner, all she could talk about was what she had learned in the books. That night, she dreamt of newborn babies and toddlers. There was no dark shadowy figure.

Chapter 23

Travis was on patrol when he was flagged down by a young man in camouflage near the highway. He stopped and rolled down his window.

"Somethin' wrong?" he asked.

The boy looked like he had just finished the 100-yd dash.

"Chief, my buddy and I found bones in that ravine over there when we were deer huntin'," he gasped. He paused to catch his breath. "They are scattered all over! You gotta come!"

Travis said, "Hop in. Show me where."

"You might better park. You cain't drive there, Chief."

So he parked and they started hiking. It took them about 30 minutes to reach the first bone. It looked like a human arm bone. Just as the boy said, there were a trail of bones stretched over maybe a quarter of a mile, deep in a ravine. The other hunter was waiting at the end of the trail.

"I think this is the last of them, Chief," he said. "I done been lookin' all over the place and couldn't find any more. I didn't touch any of them."

"Good job," Travis said. "You boys can go on home now. This is a crime scene."

After the kids left, Travis began taking pictures of where the bones lay. It was clear that the wild animals had stripped off all the meat. He could see teeth marks on them. Travis knew it was a woman's body. He had seen enough during his military service to know it wasn't a man. The bones had been bleached by the sun which told him they had been there several years.

He stood up and surveyed the terrain. It was one of a thousand ravines in this area and they all looked the same. Red dirt, scraggly bushes, rocks, steep hillsides. This particular one was about twenty feet wide and fifty feet tall. It was November and the floor of the ravine was covered with fall leaves. It was a surprise that anyone would have found these bones. He began climbing the nearest wall of the ravine. He had to get to the top to get a bearing on where he was. It was what is sometimes called a shoe-string hike. He stared at his shoe strings all the way up because of the steep incline. Travis was panting when he reached the top and stood on level ground. After taking a moment to catch his breath, he straightened up and looked around, trying to think of who owned land along this side of the highway. All he could see was trees and gullies. There was no sign of a house nearby. He hiked back to the highway, emerging from the woods a good half mile from his vehicle. He retrieved a cardboard box from his crime scene kit along with some gloves. He needed to retrieve the bones and send them to Jackson to see if they could match DNA to a missing person. He didn't have much hope. Mississippi was behind the curve when it came to high tech forensic measures. Maybe his buddy, George, could help again. It was worth a try.

It was near dark when Travis got home. He had been very meticulous as the crime scene, photographing every angle of every bone. He had put each bone in a plastic evidence bag, correlating where it had been found with the crude map he had drawn. He hadn't wanted to miss any clue that might tell him who this poor soul was. By the time he finished, it was too late to catch the courier.

The next morning, Travis shipped the box overnight to George and then called him to explain.

"Hey, George, this is Travis Hampton," he said.

"Travis! How's that beautiful little girl doin'?" George asked.

"Just fine. She's doin' great in school and is excited about...the baby," Travis stammered. He had just remembered he hadn't yet shared the news about the new baby. They spent about five minutes with small talk before they got down to business.

"Listen, I just sent you a box overnight," Travis said. "It contains human bones of a girl some hunters found in a ravine out here. I was wonderin' if you could use your influence at the state lab to pull some DNA to try to identify her."

George was silent for a moment. "I'm real sorry to hear that, Travis. You think it was foul play?"

"I can think of no reason why she would have been in that ravine alone," he said. "The animals had been at her and she's been there a few years, so it's hard to tell. I'm hopin' your forensic coroner could have a look and tell me how she died."

"Well, I'll look for the package and put a rush on it. Sure don't want the parents to suffer any longer than they have to," George said.

"That's just it," said Travis. "No one has reported anyone missin' to me. I'm gonna to do some more investigatin' here. I'd appreciate any help you can give."

"Sure thing, Trav. Kiss those pretty girls for me, okay?"

"Will do, George. Take care."

Travis was pretty sure the bones were those of one of the prostitutes that worked the bars around town. He had no problems with the poor souls who had to sell their body to live. He did have a problem with the men who abused them just for jollies. He would make his rounds to the bars as soon as they opened and the girls got out to work.

In the meantime, he pulled the county map down from the wall and studied it. He pinpointed the ravine where the bones had been found. There were very few houses in that area because the terrain was so rough. The nearest road, other than the highway, was 1100S. He remembered from Tess' case that there were only a few shacks on that road and they were all owned by meth addicts. He couldn't see any of them visiting, much less harming, a prostitute. Of course, Earl had lived on that road. His place was abandoned now since he had been in prison for five years and had many more years to go. Perhaps someone had taken one of the girls there for a little privacy. He shook his head. No, the girls were too busy to go all the way out there for a john. They would be losing money. No, it had to be a disposal sight only. He hung the map back up and stuck yellow push pins where each bone had been found. He then stuck red push pins to mark all the houses within ten miles of the crime scene. He would check them out later. Right now, he needed to interview the hookers.

It took three days to visit all the bars around and talk to the staff and the girls. Was there anyone who went missing about several years ago? Do you know what happened to them? Did they have any kin folk who might know? At the end of the three days, he had four names. Ida Mae Williams, Rosemary Jarvis, Susie Teasdale and Jody Collier. None of them had kin left in the area. No one knew where they went. They each came up missing one day, never to be heard from again. It wasn't uncommon for hookers to go missing and not be reported. Sometimes they had moved on. Sometimes they got lucky and got out of the life. If the girl was not a hooker and had come from a fine upstanding family, Travis knew there would be an uproar until she was found. That is how he knew it was a hooker. There had been no fine upstanding citizens reported missing in the last ten years.

Researching the various databases at a law enforcement officer's disposal, Travis quickly discovered some answers. Ida Mae was a petite brunette who had worked the cotton mill area. She had married one of her customers and moved to Arkansas.

Apparently, she was happily married, had two kids and was a hair stylist. Rosemary was a high end call girl. She didn't walk the streets. Her customers called her to book an appointment. Very civilized. She had found religion, married a preacher and moved to Merigold, Mississippi. Susie Teasdale had been hooked on meth and wasn't as choosy with her customers as the others. She had been murdered out behind one of the casinos in Tunica a year or so ago. The only one unaccounted for was Jody Collier.

The trailer Jody grew up in had burned years ago. And there had been no trace of her at Earl's. The only way to determine if they were Jody's was to compare the bone DNA to Jody's mother, Faye. Travis picked up the phone and dialed the town judge, Judge Dobbs. He didn't have a clerk. He always said he preferred to do his own clerking because it let him keep a better handle on the goings on.

"Judge Dobbs," he said, answering his own phone.

"Good mornin', Judge. This is Chief Hampton. Do you have a minute?"

"Sure thing, Travis. Whatcha need?" Judge Dobbs liked to keep things on an informal basis.

"I want to exhume a body to test for DNA. Some bones were found in the gullies out by the highway and

I think I know who it is, but I need DNA to confirm," Travis explained.

"Well, gosh darn it! I hate to hear that, Travis. Who do you think it is?"

"Jody Collier. She was a young girl who worked the bars around town and just came up missin' one day. Faye Collier was her mother. She died in a fire several years ago."

"Have you conducted an extensive search to try to find her without DNA?" Judge Hobbs asked.

"I have, Judge," Travis replied. "I found four girls missin' mysteriously. Three of those turned up elsewhere. Jody Collier is the only one I can't find. I've had bulletins out for months and called every police station in the state, all to no avail. If I exhume her mother, Faye Collier, I can compare DNA to see if it's Jody. There's no family to ask."

"That's good enough for me. Drop by this afternoon and I'll have the order ready."

"Thanks, Judge," Travis said, as he hung up the phone.

He stood up from his desk and stretched. He was bone weary. He had handled murder cases before, both in Jackson and in the military. None of them were as important to him as this one. Tess' future hung in the balance, as well as his and Beth's.

Travis went home for lunch. Beth had left him a plate of last night's supper, meatloaf, mashed potatoes and corn. He stuck it in the microwave and reheated it. It tasted just as good as it had last night. After rinsing his plate and putting it in the dishwasher, he went down the hall to Tess' bathroom. They had let Tess decorate it for the most part. The walls were painted pale pink. Beth had spend days stenciling tiny magenta and white cherry blossoms randomly all over. The floor was white tile and covered with dark pink fluffy rugs. The towels were pink and white. It was a very girly bathroom. Everything was so dainty, Travis felt like an overgrown ogre just stepping into it. He picked up Tess' hairbrush and pulled a few blond strands from it. He dropped those into a plastic evidence bag and put it in his pocket. He would send these along with Faye's DNA for comparison.

Travis stopped by and picked up the exhumation order on his way back to work. He called the coroner and arranged to have it done the next morning.

It was late November and the Mississippi morning fog hung low to the ground at the cemetery. There was a bone-cold chill in the air. This was an old cemetery. Some of the crumbling headstones dated back to 1901. Faye was interred in the pauper's area since no one had claimed her body. Her marker was a plain 4"x8" marble stake with a number on it, 842. Travis arrived before the coroner. He stood with his coat collar turned up to keep the chill off his neck and had his hands shoved deep in his pockets as he watched the cemetery worker carefully dig the grave out with the excavator. By the time the pine box in which she had been buried was uncovered, the coroner had arrived with his black hearse. The cheap pine box had deteriorated somewhat, but it held together when they placed it in the hearse. The coroner would take her back to his place and do a bone scraping to gather DNA. Then she would be placed back in the grave. Travis had arranged to have a preacher there to say a few words when she was reburied. It seemed the least he could do if she truly was Tess' grandmother. The whole exhumation took an hour at the most. Faye was reinterred that afternoon and Travis had his DNA. He sent it overnight to George. George had arranged to have all three DNA samples tested at the state police lab. Travis should have his answer in less than a week.

Chapter 24

"Chief Hampton," Travis said when he answered the phone the following Monday.

"Travis, this is George. I think you need to come down to Jackson. I just got the results on the bones you sent."

"What did you find, George?" Travis asked.

"It'd be better if you see for yourself," George replied. "I think you have a murder on your hands."

Travis said he'd be there in a couple hours and hung up.

A murder? It had to be Jody. He knew Earl was capable of horrific things, but murder? He grabbed his coat, called Beth to tell her he would be late and left for Jackson.

The drive through the Mississippi Delta was long and boring. It seemed as soon as one hit the Delta, time slowed down. It had its own beauty, of course. In the late summer, the cotton plants opened to reveal white, fluffy cotton. The whole field looks like it's covered in snow. But this was November, almost December, and the cotton had long been picked. The plants were dead and stood in the fields like forgotten soldiers, drooping and decaying. The fields of rice were no longer that luscious bright green color. Instead they were bare, just the rice levees standing there, awaiting next season. The whole Delta was drab and depressing. It was the poorest area in the country.

As he left the Delta, the landscape became more interesting. There were rolling hills and nicely maintained interstates. The farms along the interstate raised livestock, soybeans, cotton and chickens. Jackson itself sits atop an extinct volcano. It is the only state capital to do so. The peak of the volcano is 2900 feet directly below the Mississippi Coliseum at the state fairgrounds, although most Mississippians are not aware of this fact.

Travis pulled into the state police parking lot and hour and a half after leaving Gnaw Bone. George was waiting for him. They went to George's office and

George pulled a file from the desk drawer. He spread some photos across his desk.

"Here's what we found," he said. "Most of her bones have been disarticulated. They were literally ripped apart at the joints." He pointed to one photo.

"See this crack in the bone? That is a spiral fracture of her left tibia. And this one? It is her ulna, cracked completely in half. Her arms were ripped from the shoulder sockets. Her hips were both broken. This poor girl went through brutal trauma before dyin'," George said. "This was definitely a murder."

Travis looked in horror at the photos. How could something like this happen in his town and no one know about it?

"What could have caused this, George?"

"The forensics team thinks she was dragged behind a vehicle or whatever, for some distance. It's the only thing that explains the disarticulation," George replied.

"Any idea how long ago this happened?" Travis asked.

"They put it at about four years ago. Does that help any?"

"Not really," Travis said. "If it's who I think it is, no one knows how long she's been missin'. Anythin' on the DNA?

George perked up at that question. "I just got it this mornin'. Seems there is a familial connection between the three samples. The forensics team thinks the bone sample you sent belongs to the mother of the poor girl in these photos. The hair indicates the deceased is the mother of whomever the hair belongs to. Would that be Tess, by any chance?"

"It is," Travis replied. He proceeded to tell George the whole story of Faye, Jody and Tess, as he knew it. "At least now we know that Jody was Tess' mother and that she is dead. Sad as that is, it clears the way for us to adopt Tess."

George slapped him on the back. "I'm happy for ya, man. At least something good came of all this."

Travis left Jackson with a copy of the file and DNA results. Oddly enough, he wasn't joyous as he had thought he would be. Yes, he was happy that the adoption could now go through, but he was equally sad that Tess had lost her mother in such a brutal way. He didn't know if he should tell her the details. He pondered this on the drive home.

It was late when he got back home. Once again, Beth had left his supper warming on the stove. She came into the kitchen as he sat in the dark eating. When she flipped on the light, he could see her hair was tousled and her eyes were drooping from sleep. Yet, she was a vision. He always marveled at how she could look so beautiful in any circumstance. She leaned over and kissed him on top of the head.

"Rough day?" she murmured.

He nodded. He wouldn't discuss his findings with her tonight. It could wait till morning.

The next morning, he told Beth the whole story, all the details. They then discussed what to tell Tess. Both agreed it was best to leave out the horror of her mother's death. They would tell her that evening.

Tess took the news quite well. She hadn't known her mother, but she was curious about her. She had already suspected she was dead, so this news just confirmed it. She was quite mature at age seven. She asked Travis all sorts of questions. How did she die? And when? Where did you find her? Why was she out there? Who did it? Was it the man, Earl? Did he hurt her?

Travis answered all her questions as best and as truthfully as he could. Except for the last one. He told her that Jody had not suffered. That her death was painless. He didn't know who did it, but he promised to try to find out. Tess was satisfied.

"What's gonna to happen to me now?" she asked.

Beth answered. "Well, you know, Trav and I have been talking. How would you feel if Travis and I became your real parents?"

Tess smiled and nodded. "I think I would like that very much!"

They all hugged each other. Travis suggested ice cream to celebrate. Everyone agreed and they piled in the car. It was a happy end to a sad night.

Travis knew he didn't have much of a chance proving Earl had killed Jody. Too much time had passed. Evidence would have been washed away or decayed. He drove out to Earl's old place. He had tried to seize the property and truck as part of criminal proceeds, but he couldn't prove where meth was made, nor could he prove he had made any money selling it. Earl had no bank account. Travis had tromped all over that property, up and down ravines, looking for the lab. There were just too many nooks and crannies. So, Earl had kept his possessions. No one had dared touch anything while Earl was gone. Earl's big black truck was still sitting where he had left it. The house was undisturbed. It was as if the whole place was trapped in a time capsule. No one wanted to be on Earl's bad side when he returned. Some of the neighbors had taken it upon themselves to protect the place in hopes that Earl would show his appreciation with drugs when he got out. Old Red had run off several carloads of teenagers looking for a place to party. Red was standing in the middle of the road holding his shotgun when Travis pulled up. Red walked to the driver's side window.

"Whatcha doin', Red?" Travis asked.

"Just lookin' out for things, Chief," he replied. "Where ya goin'?"

"Well, Red, that's really not any of your business, now, is it?"

"I'm lookin' after things until Earl gets back," Red said, standing a little taller.

"That's mighty neighborly of you, Red. I'm sure Earl will appreciate that. But I have business at Earl's. Don't make me arrest you," said Travis.

"Naw, that's all right, Chief. You go right ahead. Just don't mess anythin' up," Red said. He stepped away from the truck. "Let me know if you need any help."

As he traveled down the road, he noticed the other neighbors sitting on their porch or out in the yard, all with shotguns. Travis couldn't help but think that had they been this vigilant five years ago, Tess would never have had to live through that trauma.

He parked beside the truck. If Jody had been dragged, it had been by this truck. He went over every inch of the truck looking for any sign of Jody. There was nothing. The torrential rains of several spring seasons had throughly washed away any outside evidence. Travis doubted that Earl had ever let Jody inside the truck, but he scoured the inside anyway. No luck there either.

The inside of the house looked the same as the day he had arrested Earl. Nothing had been disturbed. Red was doing a good job guarding it. He went room to room and found zero evidence that anyone other than Earl had ever lived in the cabin. He spent the rest of the day searching outside and in nearby gullies, all to no avail.

On the way back to town, Travis decided the only way to connect Earl to Jody's murder was for him to confess. He wasn't sure he could make that happen, but he'd run over to Parchman tomorrow and talk to Earl. Maybe he'd get lucky.

Chapter 25

Travis had been to Parchman prison many times since
he became chief of police. It was not a place he enjoyed
visiting. As he pulled up to the gates and showed his
credentials, he thought how awful it must be to live in a
place with no privacy, no solitude, and with men who
would rather kill than talk. There's little wonder why
men who go to prison are rarely rehabilitated. They just
become different men, meaner and more vicious. He
asked the guard if he could see the warden. The guard
directed him to the administrative building and called
ahead to alert the warden that he had a guest.

Warden Jones met Travis at the entrance. Standing
5'5" and weighing close to 200 pounds, Jones didn't
look like much. Every time Travis had seen him, he had
been wearing a wrinkly,

white suit with a white straw hat to cover his balding head. Today was no different. He was constantly sweating and wiping his forehead with a white, embroidered handkerchief.

They exchanged a hearty handshake before the warden slapped Travis on the back.

"Boy, it has been a while, huh, Travis?" he laughed.

"It sure has, Warden. I try to avoid this place as much as possible. No offense," Travis said.

"Aw, hell, no offense taken! Even I wouldn't be here if it wasn't necessary. What can I help you with?" Warden asked.

They had entered the warden's office by now and Travis settled in the overstuffed leather chair across from Jones' massive desk. The office was well appointed, with dark rich wood and leather furniture. There was a large, Mediterranean rug on the floor and brass lamps scattered around the room. The walls were lined with bookshelves containing books on every subject imaginable. The whole environment was warm and friendly. Travis found this a bit unusual for a warden's office. He supposed it calmed prisoners down and made them more cooperative to be in an atmosphere like this as opposed to the hostile environment they lived in.

"I'm wonderin' how Earl Fields is gettin' along," Travis said. "I'm lookin' at him for another crime."

"Is that so?" Jones asked. He walked over to a massive file cabinet and pulled out a thick manila folder. "What sort of crime?"

"I'm not sure yet, Warden," Travis replied. He didn't want word getting back to Earl that he was suspected of murder.

"Well, his file is pretty thick," said Jones. "He's been in some fights where a couple people were killed, but we couldn't prove who did the killin'. I know he has whipped his dorm in shape. I rarely get complaints from the prisoners in there. The guards tell me the inmates there all follow Earl without question. I don't know if it's fear or respect, but it seems to be workin'. He's up for parole in about five years and if he keeps his record clean, I won't have any problem supportin' him."

Travis sighed as he looked over the file. It was all true. Earl had been a model inmate. After the first few fights when he first arrived, there was nothing that indicated violence.

"Warden, do you know that he mutilated and tortured a three-year-old girl for years and, I think, killed her mother?"

Jones shook his head. "No, Travis. He's here on a drug beef. There's nothin' about torture or murder here!"

"That's because I couldn't prove it. Just like you can't prove he murdered those inmates. But I guarantee you he did," Travis exclaimed. "He cannot be released on parole!"

"Now, Travis, you know the parole board goes only by what's in his file. Who knows? Maybe he'll screw up in the next few years. Anythin' can happen," Jones said.

Travis tried to calm himself. "Well, I drove all the way here. Would it be possible for me to interview him?"

"Sure thing!" Jones said jovially. "I'll get him in an interview room for you. Anythin' else?"

Travis shook his head and shook Jones' hand. Jones led him down to a room marked Interview A and showed him where the coffee was. Travis waited about ten minutes before two guards brought Earl to the room in ankle and leg chains. Although he had been incarcerated three years, Earl hadn't changed much. His face was just a bit harder and his body was a little bit leaner, but he was still the mean bastard that Travis knew. The guards seated him across the table from

Travis and hooked his chains to the eye hooks on the floor and table. They left the room and closed the door.

"How you been doin', Earl?" Travis asked.

"Oh, you know, Travis. Gettin' along," Earl replied with a sneer, rattling his chains. "What you doin' down this way? How's our little girl doin' anyway?"

Travis stared hard at Earl and pressed his lips together to try to control his temper. Earl smiled. He could tell he had gotten under Travis' skin.

Ignoring Earl's questions, Travis said, "I'm lookin' into the murder of Jody Collier, Earl. What do you know about that?"

That wiped the smile off Earl's face. He leaned forward and said, "I done told you, Travis. I ain't heard from Jody in years. I mean years!"

"Well, see, Earl, that don't track. I found her remains on your property back in the ravines."

He watched as indecision flitted across Earl's face. He was frantically trying to come up with a story.

"I ain't been there for three years, as you well know. No tellin' who's been trespassin' all over my place," Earl declared.

Travis slowly nodded. "She's been there five years, Earl. They ran some tests down in Jackson that told me who she was and how long she'd been there."

"Yeah, well, you cain't prove I put her there. No way," Earl said. He relaxed a bit and sat back in his chair, an insolent grin on his face. If Travis had proof, he'd be arrested already.

"Oh, I'll prove it." Travis stood up to leave. "I don't quit, Earl. You know that." He turned toward the door.

"You didn't tell me how our girl was doin', Trav," Earl whispered.

Travis whirled, took one long stride and punched Earl in the face. "She's not *our* girl. Don't ever mention her again!"

Earl laughed out loud. "Just don't forget. She was mine first."

Travis hit him again and again until the guards burst in and pulled him off.

The one guard looked at Earl and then back to Travis and said, "So, self defense, huh?"

Travis nodded.

"Well, Earl," the guard said. "That'll get you some solitary time. Attackin' an officer is serious." Both guards chuckled.

Earl laughed as the guards led him away. He called over his shoulder to Travis, "Till next time, Chief!"

Chapter 26

Beth woke Travis up in the middle of the night in late February. She had been having contractions all night and now it was time to go to the hospital. Travis jumped out of bed, wide awake. He quickly dressed and helped Beth get dressed. Tess stood at the door, yawning.

"What's goin' on?" she asked.

"Get dressed, Tess," Travis yelled. "The baby is comin'!"

"But it's too early," said Tess. "It's not due until April."

"Tess! Get dressed!"

She ran back to her room and hurriedly dressed. Nothing matched. Striped blouse, checkered pants,

mismatched socks. She didn't care. The baby
was coming!

She threw her coat on and grabbed Beth's hospital
bag while Travis helped Beth in the car. Travis flipped
on the siren and lights and made the hour long drive to
Bolivar County Hospital in twenty minutes. The interns
wheeled Beth into the delivery room while Travis filled
out paperwork. Tess stayed with Travis, anxiously
looking down the hallway where Beth had disappeared.

When they were ready for him, the nurse led Travis
to the delivery room and gowned him up. Tess thought
he looked like one of those mad scientists in the
movies. She giggled. Travis knelt down.

"Tess, honey," Travis said. "I'm goin' to be with
Beth so you sit out here and I'll come get you when the
baby's here. Okay?"

"But, I haven't decided if I want a brother or
sister yet!"

"Well, sweetheart. I think God is decidin' that for
you right now," he chuckled. "Be good, now."

Tess sat in the hallway for what seemed like
an eternity.

Travis held Beth's hand while she breathed and
pushed. They had decided to have a natural childbirth
with no drugs. Beth was blaming him for that decision
now, although he knew she didn't mean it. He just held

on and tried not to grimace when she squeezed his hand too hard.

Labor didn't last but maybe twenty minutes. The baby popped out, a boy, and everyone breathed a sigh of relief. Even though he was a month early, he was perfect. There was no indication of underdeveloped lungs or the other issues preemies sometimes had. After the nurses cleaned him up and bundled him in a blue blanket, they lay him on Beth's chest. He was beautiful with a full head of black hair and wrinkled skin. The doctor told Travis to go tell Tess while they cleaned up the afterbirth.

Travis stepped out into the hallway and Tess ran to him.

"It's a boy," he said happily. "You have a brother!"

Tess hugged him and started crying. She was so happy.

A nurse stuck her head out the door.

"Mr. Hampton, you better get back in here," she said and disappeared.

Travis hurried back to Beth's side.

The doctor was just handing a second baby to the nurses. Twins? They had twins?

"Congratulations again," said the doctor. "You also have a daughter!"

How could this be? There was no indication on the sonograms of twins.

The nurses lay the second baby on Beth's chest. Both children were perfect. The girl, too, had a full head of black hair. The only difference between them was their gender. Travis took a moment to absorb the moment before kissing Beth on the forehead.

"I gotta go tell Tess," he whispered.

He could see Tess was worried when he saw tears in her eyes. She had read all those childbirth books and knew some of the things that could happen. He felt a sudden rush of guilt over leaving her out there imagining all sorts of things. He took his mask down and smiled.

"No worries, Tess," he said. "You'll like this surprise."

He led her back to the bench and they sat down.

"You have a little brother, right? And that makes you happy?" he asked.

Tess nodded.

"Well, now you have a little sister, too! Does that make you happy?"

Tess's eyes got real wide. A sister?

"Twins?" she asked quietly.

Travis nodded.

"Twins!" she exclaimed. "Twins! A boy and a girl! Oh, Travis, that's perfect!"

She jumped up and gave him an exuberant hug. "When can I see them? Is Beth okay?"

"Beth is fine," he said. "They are goin' to get her in the room, give the babies a checkup and then we can see them. Can you stay here just a moment more so I can tell Beth we are goin' to the cafeteria?"

"Okay," Tess replied as she giggled and settled in the bench once again.

Tess got a bowl of mac and cheese while Travis grabbed a Danish. They sat there about twenty minutes talking mostly and eating very little. They were too keyed up to finish the food. When the nurse told them the room was ready, they both raced upstairs. Beth and the babies were already in the room. There was lots of hugs and kisses for the first few moments. After much debate, all three decided to name the babies Jacob and Samantha. Tess was already calling them Jake and Sam. She held each baby as long as she could until they started fussing. When Beth took them to breastfeed, Tess curled up in the chair and fell asleep. Travis watched Beth as she fed the babies. She was glowing. Her eyes were full of love as she watched them suckle at her breast. They were tiny enough that she could feed them both at the same time. When feeding time was over, Travis kissed Beth and the babies goodnight, gathered Tess in his arms and took her home. Everyone needed a good night's sleep.

Tess woke Travis up early the next morning wanting to go to the hospital.

"Tess, honey, it's a school day. You have to go to school," a sleepy Travis replied.

"No! I want to go to the hospital!" Tess cried.

"I tell you what. You go to school and I promise you they'll be home when you get out. You can play with them all night," Travis said.

Tess pouted for a few minutes before going back to her room to get dressed. She didn't like it but she could see how tired Travis was and didn't want to add to his worries. She could wait a few hours to see her new siblings.

Tess fell in love with the babies and was always changing diapers, feeding them, playing with them. She was a great help to Beth. She was more of a second mother than a big sister. Jacob grew faster than Sam, but they were both healthy. Tess was extra protective of Samantha because she was smaller than Jacob. As their individual personalities began to develop, Travis and Beth could see Tess' influence on them. They were independent and kind souls, like Tess.

When the twins were three, Tess began teaching them jiu-jitsu. Of course, their attention spans were short and they were definitely uncoordinated in their movements, but they did master some of the basics. The family would be watching television when suddenly little Jake would jump up and challenge Sam to a match. By the end of the match, the whole family was rolling on the floor in laughter.

One night, after putting the twins to bed, Tess stood over them, watching them sleep.

"I will never let anythin' happen to either of you," she promised. "I promise to keep the dark shadows away."

Chapter 27

Tess had made lots of friends at school. She excelled in her classes and in sports. She ran track and played volleyball. All her teachers loved her. The whole town had pretty much adopted her once her story became known. Everyone protected her as if she was their own. She helped out sometimes at the little five-and-dime store in town, working behind the candy counter. The owners overlooked her habit of "rounding up" when it came to children buying candy, especially with Jake and Sam. She always gave them just a little bit more.

At age 12, she had attained her black belt in jiu-jitsu. Although, the jiu-jitsu governing body requires a student to be at least 19 years old, Tess' skill and dedication had earned her a waiver. Although she was the best on the mat, Travis knew she also needed real world experience if she was going to be able to defend herself. Sometimes, they would practice street fighting in the back yard. Travis' skills as an Army Ranger came in useful against Tess' black belt techniques. Tess' was eager to learn. Although Earl had been out of her life for seven years, she still had this inner drive to protect herself. During her training with Travis, he had drilled into her that her skills were only meant to defend herself and others. They were not to be used aggressively. She was never to instigate violence, only defend against it.

Tess knew by now that her grandmother, Faye, had traded her and her mom, Jody, to Earl for drugs. Travis had told her the details when she was eight, just after the twins were born. She didn't understand how her grandmother could do that, nor could she understand how Earl could be so evil. She vowed to never let such evil touch Jake or Sam.

Jake and Sam were three years old and had totally different personalities. Jake was a quiet, kind child. He always deferred to others if push came to shove. Not that he was timid. His skills in jiu-jitsu, even at his age, were impressive. He was a mini-Travis, with his dark hair and blue eyes. He idolized his father, mimicking his walk and trying to mimic the way he talked. When Travis was home, Jake never left his side.

Samantha also had Travis' dark hair and blue eyes, but her personality was exactly opposite. She had Beth's bubbly, happy-go-lucky attitude and Tess' fierce spirit. Even though she was smaller, she had unconsciously taken on the role of protecting Jake. She didn't let any of the other kids take his toys at day care or abuse him in any way. She didn't use violence against them, but the other kids knew not to mess with her.

No one knew when Tess' birthday was, so Beth told her to just pick a day and they would celebrate. Tess picked May 15th. Every year Travis and Beth would throw a big birthday party for her in the park and invite all her friends from school and the town. Tess didn't like to be the center of attention, but she went along with it because it made Travis and Beth so happy. But she insisted there be no gifts. Of course, everyone ignored her and brought gifts anyway. So when it came time to open them, she would pass them out to the other, less fortunate, kids who had come. The only exception was the gift from Travis and Beth. That one she kept and opened it when she was alone. Those were the gifts she treasured.

Her twelfth birthday fell on a Saturday. Tess was excited. This was the first time her birthday had fallen on a weekend. The whole town had been in a festive spirit all week. Her birthday had actually become a community celebration day of sorts. Businesses shut down early. Families brought picnics. There were games, balloons and clowns creating those little twisted balloon animals. Ribbons were hung all around the park. Jake and Sam rode their tricycles in the kiddie parade. In the evening there would be a small fireworks show.

May 15th was Tess' favorite day of the year.

Chapter 28

Earl had been in Parchman for seven years. His records show no write-ups because inmates and guards alike were too afraid to report him. So when he came up for parole, the parole board saw a perfect inmate, one who had been reformed. He sat before them and pledged to forego his evil drug dealing ways. He said he had found God while incarcerated and would live a clean, godly life. With prison overcrowding and Earl's lies weighing heavily on their decision, the board granted him parole. He was released in the early morning with a $20 stipend and a bus ticket to Gnaw Bone. It was May 15.

Earl gazed out at the Delta as the bus rolled him toward home. The land had awakened from its winter slumber and everything had turned spring green. The crops had mostly been planted and little sprouts were budding up from the rich, fertile ground. The spring rains were over and the air smelled fresh and clean. Earl noticed none of this. His thoughts were on revenge. He wasn't really angry at Travis. Trav was just doing his job. It was the girl, Tess, they called her. If she had just done what she was supposed to, he wouldn't have lost seven years of his life. Doing time hadn't really been that bad. He had established dominance after the first couple of months and then his world was good. But that wasn't the point. He would have to rebuild his meth business. He figured his house had been taken over by vagrants and who knew if someone had discovered his lab by now. He didn't like uncertainty and he didn't like change. All in all, he was not in a very good mood, despite being free. Plus he was horny. Prison sex had been good, for him at least, and plentiful, but he was definitely ready for a female.

Earl had the driver drop him at the road leading to his house before the bus ever entered Gnaw Bone. He had trekked about a quarter of a mile when he was met by a bony old man with a shotgun.

"Hold up there, stranger," the man said. "Ain't nobody allowed down this road."

Earl raised his head and looked at the man.

"Hello, Red," he drawled.

"Oh, Mr. Earl! I didn't know that as you! Of course, you can go. Welcome home! I been protecting your stuff for you till you got back," said Red.

"I appreciate that, Red. My truck still down there?"

"Yes sir, Mr. Earl! Ain't nobody touched nothin' at your place. I made sure!"

"Good. You got any motor oil and gasoline?" asked Earl.

"I think I do, out back in the shed. You want me to bring it down?" Red replied.

"Sure do, Red. Don't be long."

"Yes sir, Mr. Earl. I'll do it right now! Hop in the truck if you want and I'll give you a ride."

Earl sat in the dilapidated old truck while Earl fetched the oil and gas. He was used to people serving him. Red was no different. He knew Red was expecting dope in return and he would oblige him. It was always a good idea to keep the neighbors on his side. It could be helpful, as the last seven years had proven.

As Red's old junker rolled up to Earl's place, Earl could see his truck sitting exactly where he left it. Fine red dusk covered it so it looked rusted, but other than that, it was in fine shape. Earl got out of the truck, took the gasoline and oil, and waved Red off. There was no word of thanks or even a grunt. He ignored Red entirely, as if he were a bug about to be squished under his boot. Red didn't take offense. He knew the type of man Earl was. Narcissistic.

Earl looked over the truck and began brushing the dust off. Damn! Even though the keys were in it, no one had touched it in seven years. He was going to have to reward Red a little bit extra once he got his lab running again. That could wait. Right now he needed a car wash.

He tried to start the truck. No response. He fiddled with the battery cables and still had no luck. Well, he thought, everything can't be perfect. Of course, she needed a new battery after seven years! He should have thought of that. The old truck stop on the highway was two miles through a newly planted cotton field. It took him a little over an hour to hoof it to the station, buy the battery and get back. He had to buy it on credit because he had no cash other than the $20 the prison had given him. The manager of the truck stop knew Earl, knew his reputation and was afraid of him. He didn't hesitate when Earl asked for credit.

Of course, Earl had plenty of money buried under his house. He just didn't want to share any with the station manager. He'd rather have the battery for free. But now, he needed money to restock his lab and get things going again. He went around to the back of the house and crawled into the space right below the kitchen window. He used a garden trowel to dig about a foot down until he hit the lid of the first jar. He pulled it out. Stuffed inside were a about two hundred hundred dollar bills. This will do, he thought. There were about fifty other jars buried around the property. Only he knew exactly where.

He would have to go to Jackson to buy his meth-making supplies — muriatic acid, lye, starter fluid, and some Vick's nasal inhalers. Jackson was large enough that he could visit several stores, buying a little of each ingredient at each store, and no one would catch on to what he was doing. In Gnaw Bone, there was only one hardware store and one pharmacy, so anonymity was out of the question. Everyone knew who he was. However, he would go through Gnaw Bone and get his truck washed before he went to Jackson.

It was about noon on Saturday, May 15. He had used the car wash at the edge of town and was cruising through town taking note of all the changes that had occurred since he had been gone. The town had become a charming little slice of southern life. The streets were clean and well groomed. There were lots of people milling about, half of them tourists who came in to visit the chic little shops around the square. He had already passed through the fringes of town where his customer base lived, which weren't so nice. There were balloons and ribbons strung throughout the park and the picnic tables were filling up fast with families sharing meals. It looked as if a celebration was about to happen.

Chapter 29

Tess was excited for her birthday party. The twins were just old enough to know what was going on and they had tapped into her joy. The three of them were giddy all day. It was a blessing to Travis and Beth when they arrived at the park, knowing the kids would run off some of that energy and collapse at the end of the day, spent.

It was a perfect day. Temperature was about 75° with a slight breeze. The sky was blue and had those puffy, white cumulus clouds that looked like piles and piles of soft cotton. The magnolia trees had already lost their creamy white, waxy blooms, which had been replaced by the attractive red seed pod for next year's flowers. Scattered across the lush, green lawn of the park were picnic tables covered in various colored tablecloths. Some were red and white checked, some had a

floral pattern, and others were solid. Those who hadn't
arrived early enough to get a table had spread blankets
under the trees. The informal community band had set up at
one end of the park under the pavilion. It would play
occasionally, in between partying. The bounce houses were
at the other end near the playground. Someone was roasting
a whole pig and the delicious aroma wafted across the
whole square, making everyone hungry. The balloon
animal guy had been working steadily all morning and
every little child was wearing a balloon hat of some sort.

Tess took Jake and Sam first to the balloon animal guy.
Jake wanted a giraffe for his hat. Sam wanted a butterfly.
The balloon guy worked his magic and out popped an
orange giraffe hat. A minute later, Sam was wearing a
purple butterfly hat. They ran to show Travis and Beth.
Tess started looking around for her friends.

Travis was watching Tess with a proud smile on his
face. She had become such an outstanding young lady. He
was so happy to call her his daughter. Suddenly, he noticed
her face tense up. She had sensed danger. He had started
toward her when the twins came barreling toward him
demanding to go to the bounce houses. He looked at Tess
again and she had her back to him. He didn't see any
danger. He didn't see the truck.

"All right, you little rascals! Bounce house it is!" he laughed as he scooped them up and headed to the playground.

Tess had heard the truck before she saw it. When she first heard the rumble, she instantly felt fear. She didn't know why. She just knew that sound foretold danger. When she spotted the truck parked down the street, her fear engulfed her. All her memories of that awful time flooded her mind in such a rush, it paralyzed her. She began searching for the man. She found him leaning lazily against a tree at the edge of the park, about fifty feet from her. He was wearing an insolent grin as he watched her play. He was completely surprised when she started walking toward him.

Tess was also surprised at herself when she began walking to him. The closer she got, the less fear she felt. Her fear was replaced with rage. She wanted to hurt him. But her jiu-jitsu training had taught her control. By the time she reached him, she was a picture of calm.

"Well, aren't you just the prettiest thing," Earl said as he looked her up and down. "Spittin' image of yo mama."

"You knew my mama?" Tess asked. That had caught her off guard.

"I shore did," he said. "You might say we were real close when you were a baby."

"Really? I don't remember her."

"What do you remember?" Earl asked. He was staring at her with fire in his eyes. Did she remember him at all? After all, she had only been five. How much could she remember?

"I just remember livin' with Travis and Beth. They said they found me when I was five and I've been with them ever since. They adopted me," said Tess. "But you look familiar. Did I know you before?"

Tess hadn't realized how good of a liar she was. She remembered every vivid detail of her life with Earl. But she wanted him to feel safe.

"Yeah, honey! Don't you remember? You and your mama lived with me when you were little. Me and you used to sit on the couch together and watch TV. Remember?" Earl said.

Tess heard Travis calling for her across the park. It was time to eat.

"I don't, but maybe you can meet me later and tell me about my mama," she said. "How about tonight around midnight, here in the park?"

Earl laughed at how easy this was going to be. He wouldn't mind another game with her. It would be the perfect welcome home present. He nodded.

Tess took off running toward her family. She didn't want them to know Earl was back. This revenge was hers and hers alone. She glanced over her shoulder and saw Earl pulling away from the curb.

"Hey, birthday girl, where have you been?" Beth asked. "We're ready to eat."

"I was lookin' for my friends, but they're not here yet," Tess replied.

She had never lied to them before. Travis was still watching her. Did he sense that she was lying? She felt her face flush and she turned away to get a paper plate. Just act like nothing's wrong, she told herself. When she glanced back up, Travis was busy with Jake. She felt like she had dodged a bullet.

Beth had fixed all her favorite foods for her birthday. Fried chicken, mashed potatoes, homemade bread, corn on the cob and butter cake topped with chocolate gravy. She never did like those fake store-bought cakes. There was no love in them.

They spent the rest of the day at the park, enjoying the music and games. When the fireworks were over, Travis carried Jake and Sam to the car while Beth and Tess cleaned up their picnic mess. By the time they got home at ten, everyone was ready to collapse in bed. Everyone but Tess. She had an appointment.

Chapter 30

Tess slipped out of her bedroom window about eleven o'clock. She had checked to see if Travis and Beth were sound asleep and they were, from the snores coming from their room. Travis snored like an old bear while Beth had a soft, kitty cat snore.

She had changed from her pretty, flowery birthday dress into more sensible black, knee length leggings and a plaid t-shirt. It allowed her maximum flexibility, should she need it. She had no doubt she could take Earl down, though he was bigger and stronger. She had taken down men just like him in her competitions on the way to earning her black belt. It didn't occur to her that competition fighting was much different than street fighting. Earl was a street fighter.

Earl had been busy preparing for this "meeting" with Tess. He decided not to go to Jackson. Instead he went back to his place and gathered up his tools. There was a cave back in one of the hollers that was a good size and halfway up a steep hill. He had decided it was a perfect place to play games. Especially with Tess. He didn't want Travis coming to his place and seeing sign of her after she went missing. If she never went to his place, there would be no sign.

Earl had dragged his tools, a table and a sleeping bag to the cave and set them up. He had a battery powered light that lit the entire space. It took him about two hours to build a crude wooden cage with a lock. The entrance of the cave was hidden well and hard to find. But he needed to find a way to seal it so the screams would not escape. There was no one close for miles to hear them, but an occasional hiker or hunter might happen along at an unfortunate time.

He finished his preparations around ten o'clock and headed home to clean up. He parked beside the town square at exactly eleven p.m. He saw a slim, dark figure sitting on one of the picnic tables. She was early. He smiled. She liked him. He beckoned for her to come sit in the truck. She shook her head and motioned for him to join her. He crawled out of the truck.

Tess watched him amble across the park. He had a slow, loping gait that hinted at his nimbleness. He was also cocky and arrogant. He plopped down beside her on the table.

"Hey, sweet thang," he said. "Glad you came."

She smiled, leading him on. "Yeah, I managed to get away."

Her idea was to get him to confess to killing her mama. She had a small tape recorder in her pocket and it was running. If she kept him at ease, she might trip him up.

"So how long did you know my mama?" she asked.

"Aw, sugar," Earl moaned. "Do we have to talk about old business? I wanna start some new business."

Tess shrugged. "Maybe you can. If you tell me about my mama."

"Alright, what do you wanna know?" Earl sighed.

"Well, were you boyfriend and girlfriend?"

"Sort of. You and her lived with me for a while."

"What did she look like?"

"You look like a miniature of her, sugar. Just younger," Earl winked.

"How long did we live with you?" Tess was curious as to how much he would tell her.

"Well, let's see. Jody lived there about three years and you lived there probably another couple."

"Did she leave me?"

"Aw, come on now, sweet pea," Earl cried. "You don't wanna get all depressed and shit thinkin' about this! I wanna have some fun!"

"In a minute," Tess said firmly. "Did she leave me?"

"I guess she did. I came home one day and she was gone," Earl lied.

"Did you hurt her?"

Tess could see Earl tense up at that question. His face got stern and his eyes turned almost black.

"I did not hurt her. I couldn't hurt a fly!" he claimed as he reached up to stroke her cheek.

She forced herself not to pull away from his touch. In fact, she even leaned into it a little bit. Then she sat up straight and glared at him.

"I don't believe you. I'm goin' home unless you tell me the truth," she demanded.

Earl felt a stab of rage. How dare she refuse him! But he wanted her to trust him. He wanted her alone.

"Well, I might have roughed her up a bit when she treated me wrong, but that's it. As far as I know, she could be in Memphis or Jackson. Who knows?" Earl said calmly.

Tess knew he was lying. Evidently, Earl thought she didn't know her mama's bones had been found on his

land. Enough of this cat and mouse game. It was time
for her to go home before she was missed.

She got up to leave. "Well, I guess that's all my
questions. I appreciate you talkin' to me."

Earl stood up, too, putting his hand on her shoulder.
"Hold on there, sugar. I thought me and you was gonna
have some fun!"

Tess looked at his hand on her shoulder.

"Please remove your hand," she said quietly.

Earl slid his hand down her shoulder to her arm and
tightened his grip.

"I think we got us a misunderstandin' here, sugar,"
he growled. "See, I give you information and you have
to give me somethin' in return." He started forcibly
moving her toward his truck.

Tess immediately planted her right foot and swung
around to face him. She grabbed his balls and crushed
as hard as she could. Her jiu-jitsu training had given her
a grip as powerful as a man's. Earl was shocked when
she fought back. When she grabbed his testicles, he
immediately let go of her arm and doubled over.

When he doubled over, Tess threw her knee into his
face as hard as she could. His nose began to spew
blood. She stepped back and kicked him in his gut. He
fell to the ground, moaning. Little bitch! She was

stronger than he thought. Her last kick landed hard on his jaw and the lights went out.

Tess stood over him for a few minutes and watched to be sure he was unconscious. She had fought well, just like Travis and her instructor, Keri Stone, had taught her. But it hadn't felt good as she had expected. She thought she would feel some sort of elation that she had punished the man who killed her mother. Instead, she felt shame. She didn't like hurting people, even this man. She knew her skills were supposed to be used to defend herself and others. And, technically, that's what she had done. After all, Earl had been trying to force her in the truck. But, Tess knew she had placed herself in this situation in hopes of provoking an attack. That was the source of her shame.

She left him on the ground and walked back home. She crawled back in through her window and got in bed. But she didn't sleep well. Her dreams were filled with dark shadows again. This time they were angry.

Chapter 31

Earl came to about an hour before dawn. His clothes were soaked from ground moisture. It took a moment for him to remember why he was laying on the ground in the park. As he staggered to his truck, it all came rushing back. The little bitch had taken him down somehow. This wasn't going to be as easy as he thought. This was going to take better planning. Damn her! As he lay in bed that night, he thought about his problem. He had to get her alone without anyone knowing. He couldn't have Travis connecting him to Tess. Tomorrow would be better, he thought, as he drifted off to a restless sleep.

Beth woke Tess up early the next morning to get ready for church.

"I'm not feelin' well, Beth," Tess moaned. "My stomach hurts."

Beth chuckled. "You probably had too much cake yesterday, young lady. I'll make you some tea and you can take it easy today, okay?"

Tess nodded and rolled over in bed. She felt bad lying to Beth, but she couldn't very well tell her she had been up all night, in the park, with Earl! She was asleep when Beth left her tea on the bedside table. Poor girl, Beth thought, not used to the party life. That was good as far as Beth was concerned. She preferred Tess to stay the studious girl she was. She leaned over and kissed Tess on the forehead. Then she ran out the door to the car where Travis and the twins were waiting to go to church.

Travis was shocked when Earl walked into the sanctuary and sat in the pew behind him and his family. No one had notified Travis that Earl was being released from Parchman. He'd have to check on that. Make sure he hadn't somehow escaped. Earl had a swollen nose and bruised face. It looked like someone had beat the daylights out of him. Why would he be in church? Earl was not a spiritual soul.

Earl had arrived late. He nodded at Travis as he settled in the pew behind him. He looked for Tess, but she wasn't there. He was surprised that Travis had two other children. It hadn't occurred to him that Tess had siblings.

After the service Travis caught Earl by the arm and pulled him aside.

"What are you doin' here, Earl?" he asked.

"Why, Travis, they let me out on good behavior," Earl drawled. "Said I'm re-ha-bil-itated."

"I'll be checkin' on that," replied Travis. "What happened to your face? Isn't fightin' a parole violation?"

"It wasn't me doin' the fightin', Chief. It was some whore who didn't like my advances. She sure packed a mean punch," he chuckled, rubbing his chin.

"I'll be watchin' you, Earl. If you come near my family, it won't be good," growled Travis.

Earl laughed. "Yeah, I saw you had two more little ones. Congratulations, man! The little girl is a real looker!"

Travis grabbed his shirt collar and shoved him up against a tree. The crowd milling around outside the church fell silent. They all turned to watch. Travis slowly released Earl and walked away. Earl just smiled. Mission accomplished. He had gotten under Travis' skin again. Right now, he had to take care of business. He needed to finish his shopping trip that got delayed by Tess. Things had to get back to normal.

Travis was angry that he had been caught unawares. The state should have notified him they were releasing Earl. He was also angry that Earl was back in their lives. He would have to tell Tess. The sooner she knew, the more prepared she would be.

He found Tess curled up on the sofa reading a science book. Science had become her favorite subject in school. At least for this year. Next year, it might be art. He sat down next to her.

"Tess, I have to tell you somethin', but I don't want you to worry. You are completely safe."

Tess said, "I know. I saw him at the park yesterday."

Travis was stunned. "What?! Why didn't you tell me?"

"I didn't want to ruin the day. I'm not afraid of him anymore. I'm not five. I can defend myself this time," she stated matter-of-factly.

"I think it's best if you just avoid him altogether. He has the right to live wherever he wants. I can't stop him from bein' here. But you just stay out of his way, okay?" he said.

Tess nodded. She had no intention of staying out of his way. In fact, she was going to put herself smack dab in the middle of his way. But Travis didn't need to know that.

"Okay, Travis," she said. "I'll do my best." She was fast becoming an accomplished liar.

It took Earl three days to make a soundproof door for his torture cave. He meticulously fitted it to the odd shaped opening so no sound could escape. Then he layered soundproofing material and plastic sheet to weatherproof it. He covered the outside in kudzu and vines so it would blend into the hillside. He drilled into the rock for hinges and a hasp on the outside. On the inside, he added iron brackets up high so he could bar any escape with a 2"x4" board. He would use a key lock on the outside. He placed his portable radio inside and tuned it to his favorite rock music station. Then he stepped outside and shut the door. He could not hear anything inside the cave. He had stocked it with crackers and bottled water. He had built a cage from 2"x4" lumber. He was ready. Look out, Tess, he thought. It's time.

Travis called Parchman and spoke to the warden. Sure enough, Earl had been released because of his spotless behavior record. Not one complaint had been filed against him in seven years. It was something of a record according to the warden.

Earl began showing up at all of Tess' track meets. School was out, but the track meets didn't end for another month. He loved the way her body had developed. Those long muscular legs stretching out for the run, those skimpy, tight little shorts and t-shirt, her long luscious hair flying in the wind. She was definitely a beauty. Just like her mother. And she was feisty. Just the way he liked 'em.

He hung out in front of the five and dime while she was working. He followed her home and parked down the street from her house. He was careful to stay hidden from Travis and Beth. But Tess knew he was there. She wasn't afraid of him, but she did keep a careful eye on him. The only time she felt fear was when the twins were around and he was watching. She vowed to never let him near Jake and Samantha. She didn't want his kind of evil in their world. She would protect them no matter what it took.

Now that Tess was twelve, she was old enough to babysit for an evening. Neither Travis nor Beth had seen Earl around town since that day at church, so they felt safe leaving Tess alone while they went to dinner and a movie . They would be in Cleveland for the evening. Beth had written down all the phones numbers of the restaurant and movie theater. She also left numbers for people in town Tess could call if there was trouble. She said they would be home before midnight. Tess waved goodbye to them as they pulled out of the drive.

Tess was excited to prove she was responsible enough to be trusted with babysitting duties. She had a fun evening planned with the twins. First she would make their favorite supper, spaghetti. Then they would play a game or two and after that they would watch a little Nickelodeon. Then came bath time, a bedtime story, and off to sleep. If all went well, Tess was hoping Travis and Beth would see her as trustworthy enough to go to the park by herself with friends. Since her dust up with Earl, she felt empowered. She had made her point to him — that she was no longer a child he could manipulate and hurt. She could defend herself. She was fairly certain that he wouldn't bother her anymore, even though he was watching her all the time it seemed.

Earl had entirely different plans. He had taken great care not to be seen by her parents, but he had definitely wanted Tess aware. He had thought it would throw some fear in her, but she hadn't seemed afraid. In fact, she seemed confident. Little bitch as too arrogant for her own good. Well, tonight was the night. He was going to show her she wasn't as safe as she thought. He waited until he saw the twins' bedroom light go off. From his truck, he could see her settle on the living room sofa to read. He waited another half hour to be sure the twins were asleep and then he quietly made his way to the back door. As he suspected, it was unlocked.

Most folks in the Deep South don't lock their doors until they go to bed, especially in small towns like Gnaw Bone. Travis had done a good job rehabbing the place. The door didn't even squeak when he opened it and stepped into the dark kitchen. He took a moment to let his eyes adjust to the darkness of the house. Although the house had an open floor plan, he could not see directly from the kitchen to the living room. He stayed close to the walls and crept through the kitchen and dining room to the wide opening of the living room. He was behind her, so she couldn't see him. He took the gun out of his waistband and stepped toward her. The floor squeaked. He stopped. Tess hadn't noticed, so he took another step. Another squeak. Damn that Travis! So he hadn't done such as good job rehabbing. This time, Tess turned her head and gasped. He pointed the gun at her and whispered, "Shhhhh."

Tess asked, "What do you want?"

"I want you to come with me so we can talk about your mama some more," Earl said.

"I can't leave the babies," Tess said.

"Yes, you can. Your parents will be home in a hour and they'll be fine. You wouldn't want anythin' to happen to them by refusin' me, would you?"

"Like what? You won't hurt the babies," Tess said.

"No?" Travis asked. "You don't know that. How about I take the little girl with me instead. Would that bc better?"

"No!" Tess cried.

"Then you come along quietly now. Don't want to wake the babies and have them awake and alone for another hour, do we?"

Tess was scared now. She couldn't let him hurt the twins. She didn't want to go with him, either. Maybe she could escape like she had before once she had him away from her house. She slipped on her shoes and nodded.

"Leave your daddy a note that says you're tired and to please not disturb you. Make it sound real," Earl growled as he stuck the gun in her rib cage.

Tess got a piece of paper and a purple marker.

HEY, GUYS! THE TWINS WERE GREAT. BUT I'M TIRED SO I WENT TO BED. LET ME SLEEP PLEASE. XOXOXO TESS

She put it on the kitchen table where Beth always put her purse. They left through the back door and got in the truck. Earl blindfolded her before he sped away. He had to get her to the cave before Travis knew she was gone.

Chapter 32

It was dark and foggy after they left the lights of the town. Earl was driving too fast for her to jump out of the truck. To her surprise, he turned before he reached the road he lived on. She had been sure he was taking her back to his house. But he turned onto a gravel lane about a half mile from his road. It was overgrown and thick with honeysuckle vines and kudzu. It took another ten or fifteen minutes to get to the spot Earl wanted.

"Get out!" he said and he went over to help her down.

He removed the blindfold and crammed it in his pocket. She wouldn't be able to navigate the trail with the blindfold. He shoved her ahead of him toward a small opening in the kudzu. They hiked about ten minutes down a steep hillside and over rocks. When they got to the cave, Earl removed the door and shoved her in. He looked around to see if he could spot any lights. The cave was about midway up on a steep hill covered in kudzu. No one could see it from the bottom of the ravine and the only way to access it was from the trail they had used, which was almost impossible to find. He stepped into the darkness of the cave and pulled the door closed and put the cross bar in place.

It was pitch black. Earl flipped on a flashlight and lit the kerosene lantern. A soft glow filled the cave. Tess was standing near the door with her arms wrapped around her body to ward off the chill. She glanced around the cave, noticing the crude box he had built. She didn't think it would be difficult to get out of it. Didn't he know she had learned how to break boards in her jiu-jitsu class?

"You can't keep me here. Travis will come for me," she said softly.

"Oh, he can look all he wants, but he won't find you," Earl chuckled. "Me and you have some business to take care of."

"I didn't mean to hurt you that bad. You shouldn't have tried to kidnap me!" she cried.

"Regardless, an eye for an eye," he said. "But I gotta get back. Make yourself comfortable, honey. I'll be back in a few days."

He got through the door and closed it just in time to feel her body slam against it on the inside. But there was no noise. If she was screaming, he couldn't hear it. He smiled as he turned the key in the lock. It was going to be tough waiting three days to come back. But he figured Travis would be all up in his business trying to find her, so he had to stay away. He needed to be at his cabin every time Travis came to visit.

Chapter 33

Travis and Beth arrived home to a silent house. They thought the kids must all be in bed. Beth picked up the note Tess had left and smiled. Poor girl! The twins must have worn her out for her to be in bed this early on a weekend. Travis hugged her from behind and nuzzled her neck.

"What's that?" he asked.

"Just a note from Tess sayin' she's tired and to let her sleep," she murmured.

"Ohhhh, that means it's time for a little adult time in the bedroom," he whispered.

She turned around and kissed him deeply.

"I believe that it does," she said as she took his hand and led him to their bedroom.

They were awakened the next morning to Jake and Sam bouncing on their bed and giggling wildly.

"Pancakes! Pancakes!" they screamed.

Travis grabbed them and threw them on the bed. He hunched over them, hands in the air, fingers curled like a cat's paw. "Here comes the tickle monster!" he growled and begin tickling them feverishly until all three fell back on the bed, laughing uncontrollably.

"All right, kids," Beth said, stressing the word *kids* and staring pointedly at Travis. "I'll start the pancakes while y'all get dressed for church. And wake Tess up so she can get ready, too."

Jake stopped bouncing long enough to say, "But she's not in her room, Mama."

Beth looked at Travis. He could see the concern in her eyes. He told the kids to scoot and got out of bed. He and Beth searched the entire house for Tess. Nothing. Her bed was undisturbed. Had she been gone since last night? Why didn't they check the bedrooms when they came home? Travis knew the statistics that the first twenty-four hours were critical for missing children. The kidnapper was at least eight hours ahead of them. She could be anywhere! But the first place he was going to check was Earl's.

Travis raced through town with lights flashing and sirens blaring. It was a peaceful, idyllic morning, with people dressed in their finest, heading off to Sunday School. They didn't yet know what a vile, black morning it was for the Hampton family. They would find out later when Beth began calling Tess' friends to see if they had heard from her. Then there would be a prayer circle with lots of prayers. Travis wasn't sure that would help, but he would take all the help he could get.

Travis barely slowed as he approached Earl's road. He took the turn way too fast, almost losing control of the vehicle. The truck skidded and came to a stop feet from the edge of a ravine. Travis took a deep breath and guided the truck back on the road. It wouldn't do Tess any good if something happened to him. He slowed down a bit, but the closer he got to Earl's house, the faster he went. He pulled up in Earl's driveway and slammed on the brakes. Dust from the road had filled the air, like a sandstorm. Travis jumped out of the truck and ran to the front door, pounding on it with his fist.

At first, Earl didn't answer. He had rehearsed this scene in his mind many times over the last few hours. He had to appear nonchalant if he wanted Travis off his tail. Dressed in only his boxers and a t-shirt, Earl opened the door, rubbing his eyes as if he'd just gotten out of bed. Travis was livid.

"Where is she, Earl?" he demanded as he shoved his way into the house.

He began looking everywhere while Earl appeared to be caught by surprise.

"Who?" he said. "Who ya lookin' for?"

"You know damn well who," Travis yelled. "Tess! Where is she?"

"How in the hell would I know, Travis? I ain't seen her but once since I got out!"

Travis ripped the rug off the floor and open the hatch to the root cellar. He climbed down and saw no sign of Tess. Earl had a fleeting notion of slamming the door and locking him in down there. Naw, that would bring too much attention to himself. Travis came up out of the cellar.

"I'm goin' to search your entire property with dogs, Earl. And I'm gonna to be keepin' my eye on you. You can't move without me knowin'. Best tell me where she is right now," he growled.

"I have no idea, Trav. None at all. And you can search till the cows come home and you won't find her. She's not here!" Earl cried.

Travis stomped out of the house, got in his car and drove away. Was he wrong about Earl? He hadn't seemed to be hiding anything. But Earl was devious. He had a knack for lying with a straight face. Travis suspected Earl could pass a lie detector test with flying colors. That's how psychopaths operate. They are incapable of empathy or having any type of loving relationship. Therefore, the lie detector cannot pick up on any guilt or deception. Earl was definitely a psychopath.

Earl chuckled as Travis sped off. He thought he had played the part of the innocent suspect very well. He knew Travis would be watching him very carefully over the next few days. That didn't bother him. He could wait. He was a patient man since Parchman.

Travis had parked around the bend so he could see Earl's house, but Earl could not see him. He watched the house for a couple of hours before giving up and heading back to town. He needed to get flyers and a state wide amber alert out. Although she had been missing eight hours or more, there was still a chance she was in the state. Not much of one, he admitted to himself. If this was a stranger abduction, she'd likely be over the state line into Arkansas and further. But Travis felt in his bones that Earl had done this.

After getting the bulletins out, Travis called his buddy, State Police Captain George McNeely and asked to use his dog again. George agreed to come the next day first thing. Travis hung up the phone. He had done all he could do for right now. Tess was a tough, self-sufficient little girl. She could take care of herself, he hoped, until he could find her. His gut told him she was still in the vicinity.

Chapter 34

Tess sat in the corner of the cave, her face a tear-streaked mask. She had allowed herself to feel fear and desperation for a few minutes after Earl left. Then she shook herself out of it and determination took over. It was damp in the cave. Her clothes were wet and cold against her skin. She would have to guard against hypothermia. Although it was pitch black in the cave, she didn't mind. She had grown up in the dark and had developed sort of a sonar sense where she could sense where objects were in the inky blackness. She began feeling her away around the cave until she had memorized the exact placement of the table, cage and other items in the room. Soon, she could move confidently around the room without bumping into anything.

Tess explored the door. She had to admit that Earl had done a good job on it. It fit the doorway perfectly and she couldn't find a way to dismantle it. Finally, she gave up. She sat in a corner facing the door and ate her supper of crackers and water. She only ate a little, fearful she would run out before he returned. Her memories of the room cellar were slowly returning. The lessons learned there would help her survive this.

As she nibbled her crackers, she thought about her predicament. She had a couple of advantages over Earl. She could navigate in the darkness. She doubted he could. She could fight, although he was now aware of that, so that would be no surprise. He had been rushed when he threw her in the cave and had neglected to lock her in the cage. Her plan was to attack him as soon as the door opened. He would be so surprised, she could slip out the door and lock him in before he knew what was happening. She thought it was a sound plan. She crouched beside the door and waited. After an hour passed, she relaxed and remembered he had said he'd be back in a few days. She would have to listen carefully for his fumbling at the door. She had no way to mark time, thus no way to know if a day or a few days had passed.

Earl was waiting anxiously for the days to pass. He figured three days should be sufficient for Travis to decide he had no part in the girl's disappearance. So, he stayed around the cabin, drinking and watching TV, mostly porn. The days passed slowly.

Beth had spent the first day of Tess' disappearance calling friends and townsfolk to see if they knew anything. She created a poster with Tess' picture and hung it up all over town. She and the twins rode to all of Tess' favorite hangouts to see if she was at any of them. Jake was the serious one. He hadn't said much all day, but he searched out the car window for any sign of Tess. Once he spotted what he thought was her bike and screamed, "Stop!"

"Jake, what's wrong?" Beth asked as soon as she pulled over.

"I see her bike," answered Jake, pointing toward the alley by the diner.

Beth jumped out of the car and hurried over to the bike, followed closely by Jake. But it wasn't hers. Jake held the tears back as he trudged back to the car. Sam had gotten out of her car seat and was waiting with arms outstretched. He hugged Sam for a moment before settling in his car seat. Samantha was coping with her feelings by being overly happy.

"Good job, Jacob!" she told him. "Keep lookin'! You'll find her." Then she settled back to play with her doll Tess had bought her. No one saw the tear slip over her eyelid and run down her cheek.

Travis got home long after the Sam and Jake had gone to bed. He crept into their room and kissed each of them on the head. A sob caught in his throat when Sam reached up and hugged him.

"Don't worry, Daddy. You'll find her," she whispered.

Travis hugged her tight.

"You bet I will, Sammy," he said. "I'll never stop lookin'."

He and Beth held each other close that night. They both felt the hole Tess' absence made. Neither could face the possibility that she wasn't coming home. It was a long night.

Captain George McNeely and his dog, Arman, arrived at Travis' office the next morning. The two men shook hands, but didn't talk much. George studied the terrain map of the area Travis wanted to cover. It was a large area and would take a week or more to cover. They stepped outside and stopped dead in their tracks.

About fifty people had gather outside with hunting dogs and firearms. Word had spread that Tess was missing and they were there to help. Men, women and children had gathered to join the search. Travis was speechless. He turned away from the crowd to hide the tears. George put his arm around him. Some of the men came up and patted him on the back. No one said a word. They all just waited. After a couple of minutes, Travis cleared his throat. He faced the crowd and mumbled, "Let's get to it, then."

George gathered the crowd and gave them pointers on what to look for while searching. He gave each dog handler a piece of Tess' clothing for scent. Once everyone had been briefed, they piled into pickup trucks, with Travis in the lead, and headed to Earl's cabin.

Earl was sitting on his porch when the caravan arrived. He stood when Travis walked up.

"Earl, we want to search for Tess on your property. Will you give us permission or do we do it the hard way?"

"Aw, Trav, of course you can search anywhere you want," Earl drawled. "Just don't break nothin'. But that girl ain't here."

The squadron of people and dogs spread out in all directions. Each person had a radio with which they could communicate. They were to go slow and be meticulous, examining anything out of place.

The day was already hot, nearing ninety degrees. The thermometer would hit a hundred before the day was over. Mosquitoes were thick, especially in the woods. Travis and George began searching each gully and ravine for any sign of Tess. At the end of the day, no one had found anything. Travis called off the search at nightfall, telling the crowd to meet back at the cabin at first light the next day.

It took three days to search the entire property. No one ever found a sign of Tess. Each day, Earl would sit on the porch as unconcerned as a baby. Each evening when they left, Earl would chuckle and retire to an evening of drinking. His confidence was at an all time high.

On the final day, after Travis dismissed the troops, he turned and faced Earl on the porch. He stared at him a long time.

"This ain't over, Earl," he declared. "I know you have her. If you hurt her, I will kill you."

"Bring it on, Chief," Earl laughed. "I ain't got nothin' to hide here."

George pulled Travis toward the truck.

"Come on, Trav," he said. "We're done here."

Travis got home late that night, as he had for the last few nights. Everyone was in bed. He sat in the dark on the sofa, sipping a glass filled with whiskey. All he could think of was what Tess was having to endure. Each day she was missing was another day of hell of her. He sobbed silently. He felt a warm hand on his shoulder. Beth had sat down beside him. She held him and they cried together.

Chapter 35

Old Red had watched the parade of cars and trucks running up and down the road for the last week. Earl must be in real trouble. There hadn't been this much activity for as long as Red could remember. He was curious. He would go out in the woods and see teams of people and dogs sniffing around looking for something. He wondered if Earl had hidden drugs around the property. He began looking around for himself.

He was angry with Earl. He had spent the last seven years guarding Earl's place and his truck, and he still had not received a reward for his hard work. That just wasn't right. Earl had been home with plenty of time to make some more crystal. He'd probably forgotten about Red. Red would just have to get his anyway he could.

He was tired of waiting, so he searched every day, too, not knowing what he was looking for.

When the caravan did not show up the fourth day, he crept down the road to see if Earl had been arrested. Nope. There he was, big as day, sitting on his porch as if he didn't have a care in the world. Well, then, they must have found bupkis and given up. He trudged up to the porch and sat down on a step.

"Hey there, Earl," Red said. "How ya doin'?"

"Oh, Red, I'm just peachy!"

"I saw all the commotion down here. What's goin' on?"

"A bunch of nonsense!" declared Earl. "They're lookin' for a little girl. I don't know nothin' bout no girl! I think they finally got that in their heads."

"Hope so, Earl. Hope so," Red said, shaking his head. "Listen, I was hopin' you could help me out a little bit. I'm hurtin' real bad."

"Cain't help ya, Red," Travis laughed. "I ain't had no time to get back to business. Might be a couple of weeks before things settle down with Travis."

Red stood up. With some hesitation, he said, "Don't forget, Earl, that I helped you out guardin' this place."

"Are you threatenin' me, Red, cause that won't be good for you," Earl growled.

"Naw, naw, I ain't doin' that," Red whimpered. "I just need a little help's all. I can wait."

"Don't worry, Red. I ain't forgettin' ya. Now run on home. I got stuff to do," Earl said.

Red shuffled down the steps and set off for home. He was mad. Angry. Furious, even. He was absolutely positive that Earl was back to making crystal meth. He just didn't want to honor his promise. Well, that wouldn't do! As soon as he got out of eyesight of Earl, he stopped and hid in the bushes. He worked his way back to the cabin and settled in to watch Earl.

Earl had gone inside. He could see him through the windows making a sandwich. He sat down in front of the television with the sandwich and a bottle of booze. About an hour later, Earl passed out in front of the TV. Red decided Earl was in for the evening, and went home.

For a man who had been hooked on crystal meth for many years, Red was a determined man. Like a little terrier who wouldn't let go of a toy, he would not let go of the idea that Earl had drugs somewhere. He was outside Earl's cabin at the break of dawn the next day, hidden in the bushes, waiting on Earl. He was rewarded when Earl stepped out on the porch, shirtless, sipping on a cup of coffee.

Earl was happy. Apparently, he was done with Travis and all that nonsense. Now he could visit Tess. He was full of anticipation. This would be the first time he could satisfy his needs fully since being released. He took a sip of coffee, which was actually more whiskey than coffee, and surveyed his world. The air was still crisp from the evening coolness. The bugs had not yet began their assault on his skin. It was the perfect moment of a perfect Mississippi day. He didn't see Red crouched in the bushes. He tossed out his coffee and pulled his door shut. Time to play.

He grabbed his shirt and tool bag and hopped in his truck, whistling a perky tune. As he sped off, Red crawled out of the bushes. Dang it! He couldn't follow him in his truck. Earl would surely spot him. Red decided to search inside the house for the drugs. He searched every inch of the house hurriedly because he didn't know when Earl would be back. He definitely didn't want to be caught. There'd be hell to pay. Finding nothing in or around the house, Red threw up his hands in disgust. He cursed under his breath all the way back to his trailer. He'd have to take a different tack.

Earl's trek to the cave was difficult. The cave was actually halfway up the hillside facing, but not actually on, Earl's property. The trail was narrow and overgrown. It ran alongside the edge of the hill. One misstep and he would tumble over the side. But, Earl was sure-footed. He had been this way many times. When he got to the door, he unlocked the lock and stepped inside.

Tess had heard him fumbling at the door and raced to crouch beside it. She attacked him the instant he stepped inside. Surprised, he fell down, dazed. She had used one of her jiu-jitsu moves to kick him hard in the jaw, snapping his head to one side. The bitch was strong! She leapt up and raced for the door. But Earl was quick. He grabbed her by the leg and slammed her to the floor before jumping up and barring the door. Tess had hit her head on the hard stone floor and lost consciousness.

He lit the kerosene lantern. He picked Tess up and laid her on the stainless steel table. He bound her hands and feet with duct tape. He lifted her up and hooked her bound hands over a meat hook he had earlier hung from a chain attached to the ceiling. Tess' feet were about two feet from the floor, her eyes level with his. She hung there limp and unaware. He began removing his tools from his tool bag and arranging them on the table while he waited for her to wake up. She was still out when he removed her clothes. Now she hung there naked. He sat on a stool and watched her.

Tess' body was beginning to bloom. She had small mounds as breasts. Her body was lean from school sports and jiu-jitsu. Her pubic hair looked like peach fuzz, newly grown in. He reached out and touched it. It was soft as cotton. He felt himself getting hard. He opened his pants and started masturbating. He reached a climax about the same time Tess began stirring.

Tess' head felt fuzzy. She had a bad headache and her arms hurt. She struggled to open her eyes. She was still in the cave, but it had a cozy warm light. Her eyes flew open. He was here. She began struggling but realized she was hanging in the air. She couldn't get away from him. He just smiled and slowly stood.

He reached out a grabbed her ankles to stop her swinging. He began at her feet and slowly ran his hands all over her body. When he reached her nipples, he pinched them extra hard then leaned over and bit her breasts. Tess squirmed the whole time, but did not scream. He began biting her in several places, a few bites drawing blood. All of a sudden, he pulled back and slammed his fist into her stomach. She groaned from the pain.

"You will scream, bitch," he growled. "Sooner or later, you will scream."

He slugged her again, this time in the kidney. He smiled. Damn! This bitch was just like her whoring mother, Jody. He remembered torturing Jody and she never uttered a sound because she didn't want baby Tess to hear her. He tortured her for hours and still she remained silent. Of course, Tess wasn't protecting an infant now. He knew she was too stubborn to give him the satisfaction of hearing her scream. He'd fix that. He turned to his tools and picked up the razor sharp scalpel.

Tess moaned in pain. Her body had forgotten how bad this type of pain was. It felt as if she were falling into an abyss, crashing into the sharp rocky sides as she fell. There was no light, only inky blackness. She had been hit before in her jiu-jitsu classes, but not like this. Students always pulled their punches to avoid harming anyone. There was no pulling of punches in this exercise. She was being slugged with full force.

Tess had unconsciously chosen to view this torture as an exercise. A problem to be solved. She knew she couldn't escape. She accepted that she had to get through this anyway she could. Her problem was how to bear the torture without feeling it, without screaming. Her solution was to compartmentalize so she could view it unemotionally, as if it were happening to someone else. From outside her body, she watched the scene unfold from the top of the cave.

Earl turned toward Tess with the scalpel. He placed it just below her left buttock and ran it down the back of her leg. The blade left a thin, red line of blood in its wake. Tess moaned, but did not jerk. He did the same thing to the inside of her thigh. Still, Tess showed no reaction. What the hell was wrong with this girl?! Was there no fight left in her after just a few puny punches? He guessed she wasn't like her mother after all. Her mother had never given up the fight. Tess' non-reaction made him angry. He began slashing at her wildly, albeit with shallow cuts, and everywhere but her face. Here the girl was covered in blood, dripping in pools on the cave floor, and she hadn't yet cried out. Earl was frustrated.

He lowered Tess to the floor and unchained her. He placed her on the cold, metal table. Tess appeared to be unconscious, but he cuffed her wrists and ankles anyway. He began dabbing salt on the cuts. The first sting elicited a loud wail from Tess. He continued until her body was coated in a layer of salt. Tess watched from her mental perch above as he raped her savagely. It looked to her as if he was raping an inanimate rag doll. The girl below made no sound nor movement.

Earl scooped Tess up from the table and threw her in the wooden cage he had built. The cage was barely large enough to hold a dog, much less a human being.

She would have to lie in a semi-fetal position in order to avoid the nail tips he had nailed through the entire cage. It was truly a cage of pain.

After Earl left, Tess opened her eyes and considered her options. She couldn't see any way out. If she moved the slightest, the nails would shred her already cut skin. The only side of the cage not covered in nails was the bottom where she lay. She thought she might be able to flip the cage on its side and kick out the bottom. It would be excruciating because her poor battered body would be forced onto the nails, but it was her only option. She could bear the pain to her body but she couldn't afford to maim her feet.

She began rocking against the sides of the crate. Each rock got harder and harder until the cage began to tilt. Suddenly it shifted and fell on its side, throwing Tess into the nails forcibly. She cried out in pain. She lay there for a moment to collect herself. Then she brought her knee to her chin and kicked. She had gathered all her strength to deliver a powerful kick. The 2"x4" cracked. She kicked again. This time the board broke, half of it flying across the room. Tess crawled out of the cage and fell in a bloody heap on the cold stone floor, sobbing. Her skin was on fire so the cool floor felt good. She would need to rest, to regather her strength. Tess cried herself to sleep.

Chapter 36

Earl literally danced away from the cave. His first session with the bitch had been thrilling, everything he wanted. He just wished she had reacted more. But she was stronger than he thought. He would have to hurt her bad before she screamed. Next time, the cave would reverberate with her screams. He'd see to that. He headed to the Booty Call bar to celebrate. He didn't see Red standing in the shadows as he pulled out on to the highway.

Red had heard Earl's truck start up. His trailer was right on the corner of County Road 1100 and the highway. He ran out the door and raced to the corner of the intersection. He hid in the bushes as the roar of Earl's engine drew closer. He was startled to see Earl pull out of the lane about a half mile down the highway. There was nothing down the lane. It dead ended a couple miles back. Red suspected Earl's lab was hidden down this road somewhere. It required more investigation, he thought. He couldn't take his truck because there was no place to hide it should Earl come back. He would have to hoof it. Although Red looked like a walking skeleton and was a life long meth addict, he was not a weak man. He was wiry and strong with higher than average endurance for a man his age. He hurried back to his trailer to retrieve his hiking stick and pistol. He was going to find that lab tonight come hell or high water!

Red watched for traffic as he hiked up the highway to the hidden lane. There was no one on the highway tonight. He started down the lane unobserved.

It was dark already, moonlight dancing through the leaves onto the rocky lane. The crickets were singing their mating songs and the mosquitoes were dive bombing him. The dormant raspberry bushes were thick. He couldn't avoid the scratches from the thorns. He used his walking stick to move the bushes out of his way. About two miles down the lane, he found a space where Earl had parked his truck. Old and new cigarette butts marked the spot. To the left, there was a break in the thorns where someone had obviously made a path. Red entered the brush at that point and followed the trail. It was steep and rocky. He was careful because one misstep would send him hurling down the steep hillside. Damn, Earl, he thought, you sure found a good hidin' spot for your lab. About fifty feet down, the trail leveled off into a thin flat twenty foot walk. Red got to the end of the trail and looked around. Moonlight flooded the landscape as if it were broad daylight. He saw that he was on the hillside facing his own trailer, but he could not see the trailer. There was no lab, no cave, nothing.

"That son of a bitch!" he cursed under his breath. "Led me on this wild goose chase for no good reason!"

He collapsed against the kudzu, needing to rest after that arduous trek. He felt the kudzu give way behind him. Startled, he stood up and felt around the wall. Something was wrong. Upon closer inspection, he noticed a brand spanking new Yale lock. Apparently, there was a door. Red was jubilant. He had found Earl's lab. And what a fine job Earl had done in hiding it. Kudos to Earl, he thought. The lock was sturdy. He picked up a big rock and hit it several times. It didn't break. He could shoot the lock, but he didn't know where Earl was. He was afraid Earl would hear the shot and come looking. He thought about it for a minute. He convinced himself that even if Earl was within hearing range, he could grab the drugs and hightail it home before Earl could get to him. He decided it was worth the risk.

Red pulled the pistol out of the back of his pants and fired at the lock. The lock cracked like glass and fell to the ground. He waited silently and listened for Earl's truck. No sounds. He pulled the heavy door slightly open and slipped inside. Suddenly something hit him square in the chest. He staggered back, blocking the door. What the hell, he thought. Had Earl sneaked back in somehow? He tried to stand up.

"Now, Earl, I don't mean no harm," Red squeaked. "I was just curious. Please, man, don't hit me again."

No reply from Earl. Once Red's eyes adjusted to the dark, he was horrified to see a little girl standing in front of him, stark naked and bleeding from everywhere. He realized he had seen her around town with Travis.

"Holy Mother of God!" he exclaimed. "Ain't you Travis' girl? What happened to you, child?"

Tess studied him for a moment. He was scrawny with patches of gray hair on his head. He was a meth addict. She knew from his look and his mannerisms. What was he doing here? Were he and Earl friends?

"Who are you?" Tess demanded.

"Why, I'm Red. Me and your daddy are friends," he replied.

"What are you doin' here?"

"I was followin' that bastard, Earl, tryin' to find his meth lab. He owes me! Is it here?"

He took off his shirt and handed it to the girl. She put it on, giving him a grateful glance. Red realized quickly that this cave was no lab. It was a prison.

"Can you get me out of here?"

"Why, sure! You come on with me, honey. I'll get you home. This ain't no place for a girl like you."

Red poked his head out the door and looked around. Still no sign of Earl. He motioned for Tess to follow him.

"Now, this is a hard trail. You think you can make it okay? You look like you've had a hard time," Red asked.

"I can make it. Just lead the way."

Red could barely make it back up the steep trail. He kept glancing back at the girl, but she seemed to be doing better than he was. Poor child. How could she be so strong? How could Earl be so evil as to inflict that kind of pain on her? He vowed to do all he could to see Earl pay for his crimes, even if it meant not ever getting any crystal.

Tess followed closely behind Red. She was frantic to get to the top. Earl could come back any minute. She had to get home. The old man in front of her was moving as fast as he could on this difficult terrain. It wasn't fast enough for her. They finally reached the top where Earl would park his truck. Both collapsed on the ground, panting hard. After a few minutes of rest, Beth stood and helped Red to his feet.

"We have to hurry, Red," she said. "He could come back."

"You're right, missy. Let's get a move on."

They walked about half a mile before they heard the truck and saw two headlights coming their way. Red shoved her hard to the other side of the road. She rolled about five feet through the thorns, coming to a stop at the bottom of a slight hill. Red had dived for the other side of the road, but Earl spotted him before he could hide. He revved his engine and slid to a stop right where Red had been. Red looked up to see Earl standing over him like a giant. Earl reached down, grabbed Red's scrawny arm and jerked him up.

"Whatcha doin', Red?"

"Uh, nothin', Earl," Red answered nervously. "Just takin' a night stroll."

"Why this particular road?"

"Well, you see, Earl, I ain't been down this road in a while. So, new scenery, I guess," Red gulped.

"And what did you find, Red," Earl growled and tightened his grip.

"Nothin'. Just nothin'. The path is too tangled. Couldn't get very far."

Earl pushed Red back.

"You know what, Red. I think you're lyin'. You wouldn't lie to me, would ya?"

Red looked down and shook his head. He was trembling.

"I asked you a question, Red," Earl shouted.

"Naw, Earl, I wouldn't lie to you! Please. Don't hurt me," Red cried. He began to sob.

Earl hated weaklings. He punched Red hard in the face. The old man fell down. Earl kicked him in the ribs. He continued the vicious assault until Red no longer moved. Earl reached down and felt for a pulse. Satisfied, the old man was dead, he stood up. Now to see if he had found the cave. The bitch better still be there.

Tess waited until Earl had sped off to the parking area. She saw his tail lights turn off. She waited a couple more minutes before creeping out from her hiding space and running over to Red. The poor man. She had seen the beating and knew he was dead. Tears ran down her face. He had saved her at the expense of his own life. She was the reason he was dead. She kissed him on the cheek and stood up. Earl was never going to give up on her. He would never not be evil. He would always be the monster in her dreams. She had to stop him.

Determined, she crept through the brush back to the highway. She recognized where she was and knew that Earl's cabin was down the road a bit. She hurried as fast as she could considering her injuries. If she saw headlights, she crouched in the ditch beside the road until they passed. She didn't need to be rescued.

When she finally reached the cabin, she carefully opened the door and peeked inside. No one was there. There were few places to hide. She could hide under his bed, but he would surely see her. She chose the root cellar, her "room" from long ago. Earl had gotten rid of the rug that hid it for some reason. He would never suspect her of hiding there of all places. She had just lowered the hatch when she heard the truck roar into the driveway.

Earl had been livid when he found the girl gone. He had seen the door of the cave had been pushed off to the side. Damn that Red! He lit a lantern and peered inside. That little whore! She was gone! She had been nothing but trouble since that bitch Faye had foisted Jody and the baby on him. Now he was done. He would have to kill her to get rid of her. First, he had to catch her before she made it home. He drove home slowly, searching both sides of the road.

By the time he pulled into the driveway, he had already searched every inch of the road leading to Gnaw Bone. It had taken several hours and it was almost daylight now. He would rest a bit and then head out to search the terrain. She was out there somewhere and he would find her. Seemed like déja vu, he thought, reliving the last time he had to hunt for her. Even the last time he hunted for Jody! The whole family of women was nothing but trouble for him. He should have dealt with them earlier.

Earl sacked out on the sofa with a bottle of whisky to watch a little television. Eventually he passed out, either from fatigue or the whisky. Maybe from both. When he began snoring, Tess knew it was safe to come out. It was amazing to her how fast memories of her life with Earl came rushing back. Memories she had long ago buried and forgotten. She raised the hatch just a little to peek out. There he was, on the sofa. The bottle had fallen to the floor. She raised the hatch a little at a time, until she could crawl out on the kitchen floor.

Tess crept over to where Earl lay. She waved her hands in front of his face before giving his shoulder a little nudge. Earl didn't stir. Tess scoured the cabin looking for rope or rags to tie him up with. She found some rope under the sink and bound his wrists and ankles as tight as she could. She retrieved a sheet from the bedroom and spread it out in front of the sofa. With some exertion, she managed to roll Earl off the sofa onto the sheet. Calling on all the strength she had, she pulled to sheet over to the hatch. It was only a few feet, but it took her a full half hour to do it. She pushed and shoved Earl until he fell down the hatch and landed on the dirt floor. He began moving at that and then settled down again.

She slammed the hatch closed and pushed the table on top of it. She loved the irony of it. He had kept her in there like a dog all those years and now he was there. He would be enraged when he came to, she had no doubt. But for now, he was trapped and she needed some sleep. It had been a long couple of nights. She fell asleep as soon as she lay down on the sofa. She slept soundly, with no dark shadows.

Chapter 37

The spiders were what woke Earl up. There were dozens of them crawling all over him. He tried to brush them off and that's when he realized his hands were tied. What the hell? Now all dregs of sleep were gone and he was keenly aware that he was trussed up like a pig ready to roast. How did this happen? Last he remembered, he was drinking on the sofa watching some babe give a guy oral sex.

"Hey!" he yelled. "Let me out of here!"

Tess had been watching him through the crack in the hatch. She stomped on top the hatch.

"Shut up!" she yelled. "No one can hear you, remember?"

Earl recognized Tess' voice. How had she managed to get him down here?

"You whore!" Earl shouted back. "Let me out of here! I'm gonna to kill you!"

"Well, now, Earl," she replied calmly. "That's not much of an enticement for me to let you go, do you think? You gotta be nicer than that."

"Ahhhhhhh!" he yelled and continued to struggle.

Tess was hungry. She looked around the kitchen and found some peanut butter and jelly. She made herself a sandwich and sat down to eat. When she finished, she took one slice of bread and shoved it through the crack.

"Enjoy your supper, Earl," she sang. She didn't know what to do now. She hadn't planned this far. She thought she might keep him in the root cellar for a couple of days, then walk into town and tell Travis where he was. She felt bad letting her family think she was missing, but she had to teach Earl a lesson, so he would leave her alone.

Earl tried wriggling out of his bonds, but the bitch had tied him up real good. It was pitch black in the cellar so he had to feel his way around, looking for anything to cut the rope with. Unfortunately, he had done too good a job on that day long ago when Travis had been searching for Tess. There was nothing in the cave. He did have a switchblade in his front jeans pocket. That is, if the girl hadn't taken it before she shoved him down here. He couldn't get it because his hands were tied behind his back. So he rolled onto his side and rocked until he felt the knife pressing into his hip. Ah, ha! She wasn't as smart as she thought. He lay there an hour or so, wriggling and moving, until he forced the knife out of his pocket and onto the ground. It didn't take long to squirm to pick up the knife, pop the blade open and slice the rope around his hands. Blood soaked the rope due to the minute cuts he had inflicted on himself trying to cut the rope.

After he freed his feet, Earl stood up. The cave was only six feet high and with his 6'4" frame, it was a tight fit. Tess had remembered the cellar as being huge and tall. She never would have been able to reach up and touch the hatch. She hadn't taken into account that Earl could. She was startled when he punched the hatch twice, making the table jump off the floor. She realized she needed something heavier to hold the hatch closed. The only thing she saw was a bureau on the opposite side of the kitchen. She thought she could get it pushed over the hatch while he gathered enough strength to jump and hit the door again. She still hadn't realized he didn't need to jump.

Tess ran hurriedly over to the bureau and tried to pull it from the wall. It as one of those heavy, oak bureaus. She couldn't budge it. She was trying again when Earl burst up out of the cellar in a rage. She looked for an escape. The bedroom was right next to her, so she rolled around the corner and slid under the bed. If she got a chance, she would escape through the window.

Earl didn't see Tess when he first got out of the cellar. His eyes were still adjusting to the light. There was one kerosene lantern lit, sitting on the counter. He picked it up and waved it around the room. It didn't give off very much light. He reached for the other two lanterns and lit them. Still, he did not see her in the main room. She must be in the bedroom then. He took one of the lanterns and stepped into the bedroom. There was no closet in which she could hide and he didn't see her anywhere else in the room. So he knew she was under the bed. Waiting, like the little snake that she was. He reached down and grabbed one of her feet.

He pulled her, kicking and screaming, out from under the bed. He held her up like a prize fish. She punched at him, cursing and swearing like a sailor. One of her kicks almost knocked the lantern out of his hand. He laughed. When would she learn she couldn't beat him? That he would always win?

He dragged her back into the main room. With a huge haymaker swing, he rammed his fist into her ribs. She felt one break. He threw her against the wall and she crumpled into a heap on the floor, momentarily unconscious. She struggled to stand up. He watched her stand and laughed. She wouldn't stand for long, he thought. Just as she steadied herself, he threw a kick her way, aiming for her gut. Tess grabbed his foot midair and twisted as hard as she could. That threw him off balance and he slammed to the floor. She jumped on him and began pummeling his face. Her training had given her unusual strength for her age. But not enough to defeat Earl. He wrapped his arm around her and pulled her off, holding on tight.

"So, you like to fight, huh? Just like yo mama," he snickered. "You think you can beat me?"

Tess glared at him, face full of rage.

"Well, let's give it a go, then, shall we?" he said. "We will have a proper fight!"

He threw her across the room, knocking over the table, sending everything on the table crashing to the floor. She slammed into the cabinets. The pain was excruciating. He stood her up and looked her over.

"I don't figure it's fair to finish you off while you are in this condition," he said. "Go ahead. I'll let you rest a moment before I kill you."

He stepped back a couple of steps, enjoying her pain. His final blow would be to her head and it would snap her neck. He wanted to drag out the beating just a little bit longer.

Tess was leaning against the sink, trying to catch her breath. She suspected that her broken rib may have punctured a lung because it was difficult to breathe deeply.

Earl spoke really low. "Tess? Tess, you awake?"

She raised her eyes to meet his.

"I just want you to know. When I'm done with you, I'm movin' on to your little sister. She's a beauty!"

Before he had time to finish his chuckle, Tess had conjured up enough energy to throw all her weight into a kick to his knee. She heard it crack as they both fell to the floor. She knew she had broken it as she had broken so many boards in her training. She pulled herself up and hobbled over to stand over Earl.

She looked down at his face, contorted in unbearable pain, and whispered, "You will never touch my family."

Earl couldn't believe what had happened. How had such a puny girl gotten the better of him? He lay there, writhing in a agony, as he watched her walk away. He knew he was done in these parts. He had to get out of here before she got to Travis. He reached up to grab the corner of a dish towel hanging off the counter top. He needed to wrap his knee. He pulled. The kerosene lantern that had been sitting on the towel came tumbling down, soaking him in kerosene. This time the wick held its flame and Earl was instantly on fire. An image of his sisters fighting the flames flashed in his mind. He smiled as the flames licked at his skin. The pain was delicious. How they must have enjoyed that, he thought. Then he began screaming.

Tess had hobbled only to the end of the drive before the house burst into flames. She turned to watch the fire gobble up the shabby little torture house. But she didn't linger. That man had taken too much from her. She wouldn't let him have another single moment of her thoughts.

She turned and began walking. She only had one destination in mind. Home.

Enjoy a preview of J T Daniels' next bestseller

Boy on a Shelf

Inspired by the true story of horrific child abuse and the normal people who allowed it to happen.

Available on Amazon and Kindle

Sally was grateful to be living at Mrs. Williams' house. It was the first place she had ever lived that she felt safe. Her mother's boyfriends had all been abusive. Not to her, but to her mother. They had moved from one man to another with never a place to call home. But she felt at home here. She had Macy and Joy, whom she considered sisters. She had her own bed. She was fed regularly. Those were all good things. The only bad thing was she didn't get to spend as much time with her mother. It seemed Jennifer was always busy trying to please Mrs. Williams and just didn't have time for her anymore. She always seemed to have time for Peter, though, and Sally was jealous.

Although Sally was the same age as Macy, she and Joy had developed a closer friendship. Sally began hanging out with Joy and her friends after school. She liked being part of a group. She liked being the sidekick of the group leader, Joy. To her, Joy could do no wrong.

The group had stopped coming over when Jennifer and Sally had moved in. Joy didn't want to take the chance that they would report her because of the games they played with Peter. But after getting to know her new housemates, Joy decided it was okay to let her friends come over again. Five kids showed up, money in hand, at her house that first afternoon.

Sally didn't know what would happen. She just knew she hadn't seen Joy this excited in a while. The kids each handed Joy five dollars as they entered the house and went upstairs. Sally followed the group upstairs to Peter's room. She hadn't had much to do with Peter since being there. All she knew was he was retarded, took up all her mom's time and not allowed out of his room.

Joy gave each of her friends a bit of Vapor Rub to put under their noses to ward off the stench of urine and poop. They stood in a semi circle around Peter, who was sleeping on the floor. Sally was behind them. She gasped as one of the kids kicked Peter in his stomach. He screamed, awake now. She covered her ears, but did not turn away. Another kid stomped on Peter's hand, eliciting another scream. Someone punched him in the face, busting his lip. Sally was fascinated. She had seen violence like this between her mother and her boyfriends, but never such violence committed by children on children.

The abuse continued until the ten minutes were up. By then Peter was curled up in a little ball, sobbing. Joy ushered her friends out and closed Peter's door. Sally just stood outside the door, still in shock. She wasn't sure how to handle this. The violence had excited her, but she knew it was wrong. She wasn't supposed to like it, but she did. And no one was hurt, except Peter and he was retarded so he really didn't feel it, did he? That's what Joy told her.

Sally saw Macy sitting down the hallway, tears running down her face.

"What's wrong, Macy?"

"They hurt Peter again," Macy sobbed. "I can't stand it."

Sally chuckled.

"Macy, they didn't hurt him. He's retarded. He can't feel it! Didn't you know that?"

"Really? How do you know that?"

"Everybody knows retards don't have any feelings."

Macy thought about the times she had cleaned Peter up after Joy's sessions. He had cried and winced when she touched his injuries. She was sure he did feel pain. But what if Sally was right? Could it be he was faking it just to get her attention? That was not cool. The last time she had tried to help him, he had gotten the chain. She was afraid if she helped him again, something worse would happen.

Sally took her hand. What a wuss Macy was, getting upset over something like that, she thought.

"Come on. We're going to the park now. Wanna come?"

Macy wiped her tears and stood up.

"I guess."

At least at the park, she couldn't hear Peter whimpering.

About the Author

J T Daniels was raised in Cleveland, Mississippi, and now resides in Alexandria, Indiana. This is the first of many novels to come. All feedback is appreciated. Please communicate at JTDanielsBookClub@gmail.com.

Made in United States
North Haven, CT
21 January 2025